Contents

FOR MY GRANDSON
SHANE MASON

The Real Drumshee

Often my readers ask me whether Drumshee is a real place and the answer to that is: yes, it is a real place, a small farm in County Clare in the west of Ireland, but I made up the name 'Drumshee'.

I have not been able to find out much history connected with 'Drumshee' but it is almost certain that the farm was continually occupied since the Iron Age. There is a big Iron Age fort on the top of the hill with a magnificent ditch and the remains of a high wall around it. The people would have lived in small stone houses within the walls.

At some stage, probably in medieval times, there must have been a castle built inside the enclosing wall of the fort as there are many huge, beautifully cut stones on the farm. These include some battlements from the top of the castle, possibly some of the spiral staircase and also a stone with a latch hole cut at the side of it. These stones date to the late medieval time. There is also a tiny casement window – with almost no glass left in it, except tiny pieces of greenish, bubbly glass in the corners of the metal strips that form the diamond pattern on the window. This is undoubtedly from the castle, also.

When the castle was demolished, a cottage with thick stone walls and a thatched roof (later a stone roof) was built outside the walls of the fort – and that is where I live today, on a farm of twenty acres.

If you want to know more about Drumshee, or about me, log on to www.coraharrison.com.

Prologue

And so they carried the two bodies back from Clontarf to Drumshee. They went slowly; although the man was dead, the boy was still alive.

The two bodies were carried on leather stretchers, each slung between a pair of carthorses; the riderless grey stallion was led behind the first stretcher, then came the second stretcher. And behind them came what was left of the company of men that had set out with Brian Boru from Kincora to drive the Vikings from Dublin.

The dead man was Oscar of Drumshee. And the boy . . .

'What's the boy's name?' asked Niall of Corcomroe swinging around abruptly to face young Fintan who rode behind him.

'Lochlann.'

'You were neighbours?'

'Yes,' said Fintan. 'We were neighbours; Lough Fergus is only two miles away from Drumshee. I haven't seen him for a few years, though, because he's been at Kincora with King Brian,' he added.

'About your age?'

'Yes, he'd be about sixteen?'

'So you would have known him well?'

'Yes,' said Fintan. 'I knew him. Our fathers were blacksmiths – both of them – and the families knew each other.'

'What did the healers say about him?'

'They think he has brain fever as well as the wound in his leg.'

'Will he recover?'

'They thought he might,' said Fintan carefully. 'They thought the sight of his home might rouse him.'

Niall shrugged. 'That's if he is still alive when we get to Drumshee,' he said dourly and then after a moment he added: 'Only son?'

'Yes,' said Fintan. He spoke reluctantly. He knew what would come next.

'Any sisters?'

'One,' said Fintan shortly. He could hardly bear to think of Nessa just now. He had thought of her almost continually during the last few months, of her eyes, blue like the sky on a summer's day, of her soft silky primrose-coloured hair. What would Nessa say to him when he brought to her the two bodies – her dead father and her dying brother?

Chapter 1

Dunkeld, Scotland, 1014

Lochlann of Drumshee knelt before Malcolm II, King of Scotland. He bent his knee, but he did not bend his back. He stared with pride into the seamed face of the man they called The Destroyer. Lochlann felt no fear. He was the messenger of a greater king than Malcolm. He had come from Brian Boru, and men had named Brian Boru, 'The Emperor of the Irish'.

'Your message?' Malcolm's voice was deep and guttural, the voice of a man who drank heavily.

'My Lord, King Brian Boru, asks for your help. He joins with King Malachy of Tara in his struggle against Mael Mórdha, King of Leinster, and Sitric The Viking, King of Dublin.' Lochlann spoke slowly and clearly. The Scots and the Irish both spoke a Gaelic tongue, but there were differences. He scanned the king's face carefully. Malcolm nodded. He had understood; that was plain. The small ruthless eyes were sharp with intelligence. Lochlann turned to the woman at the king's side.

'My Lady,' he said courteously. 'My king, your father, sends you his best wishes for your continued good health and happiness.'

Unexpectedly Malcolm laughed. 'Yes, yes,' he said. 'I had remembered that your King Brian was my father-in-law, but – see you – I have relations everywhere. I cannot come to the rescue of them all.'

'My Lord,' said Lochlann quickly. 'It is no rescue that my king asks for. Rather he would offer you a chance to share in the glory of this battle.'

Malcolm threw back his head and laughed. He turned to his wife. 'This fellow countryman of yours has a silver tongue, my dear – silver hair, silver tongue.'

Now it was the woman's turn to smile. She was like her father, Brian Boru, thought Lochlann. She had the same thoughtful hazel eyes, the same high forehead and long shapely nose. She was looking at him with interest.

'You are very blond for an Irish boy,' she said. 'Where do you come from?'

'I come from Drumshee in the kingdom of Corcomroe, west of Thomond,' he replied. 'My grandfather was a Viking,' he added proudly. 'He served your father, King Brian, from the time that he was fourteen years old until his death three years ago.

His name was Ivar and my grandmother was Emer of Drumshee, in the kingdom of Corcomroe.'

Her eyes widened. 'I know who you are now,' she said. 'It was your grandmother's family in Drumshee who sheltered my father before he became king. Your grandmother, Emer, was my tutor and my sisters' tutor when I was young. You serve my father now?'

'Yes,' said Lochlann proudly. 'I am one of his bodyguards.'

'You are young for that,' said Malcolm.

'I have been with him for two years now,' said Lochlann. 'He trusts me. There are ten of us. We form his bodyguard.' He thought over the ten. The faces passed through his mind, especially that of his enemy, Turlough, the old king's grandson. Turlough and he had been rivals from the time that they were both ten years old and they had both been sent to the same monastic school on Scattery Island.

But I am the one that Brian Boru chose to send on this mission, thought Lochlann proudly. He remembered Turlough's fury at the decision, and at that thought his white teeth showed in a small smile of satisfaction.

'You speak Norse?' asked Malcolm.

Lochlann nodded. 'Yes,' he said. 'I speak Norse. My grandfather taught the language to my sister and to myself, when we were children.'

'So that's why he sent you on this mission,' mused Malcolm. 'It is useful to be able to speak Norse around the coast of Scotland these days.' He spoke like one whose mind was busy considering something else. His eyes were like the points on a javelin, thought Lochlann – sharp, bright, menacing. He had ceased to think about the boy in front of him; Lochlann knew that. Now he was weighing up the consequences of helping his father-in-law. There were so many groups to take into account. In Ireland there were five or six kings. In Scotland, Malcolm the Destroyer held the balance of power over the minor kings, but the Vikings were on the islands all around him. And in England, Saxons warred with Danes and Norsemen. Lochlann held his breath. Would this first mission of his be successful? What would Malcolm decide?

'I'll send a galley with a couple of hundred men,' said Malcolm abruptly. 'I hear that Sigurd, the Viking King of Orkney, is sending dragon ships filled with men-at-arms to aid Sitric of Dublin and so is Brodar of the Isle of Man. The Vikings unite; so the Gaels must unite against the Vikings. Go now. Tell my wife's father that the galleys will be sailing up the Shannon to Limerick by Easter Sunday to join Brian Boru's army – no, we will get them there a week sooner,

11

they will be there by Palm Sunday.'

'And bring messages of love and duty from me to my father,' said the queen softly. 'Tell him that I remember Ireland. I remember the kingdom of Thomond and the palace at Kincora, and I remember Emer of Drumshee who taught me when I was a child. It was a great pleasure for me to see her grandson.'

The king rose to his feet, nodding curtly to Lochlann as he went, but the queen lingered.

'Have you any brothers?' she asked.

Lochlann bowed. 'I have but one sister, my lady,' he said. 'Her name is Nessa. She is fifteen years old.'

'And she, is she at the palace of Kincora, also?'

No, my lady,' said Lochlann. 'She remains at Drumshee. She has to . . . she cares for my mother who is b. . .blind.' He stammered slightly over the word blind.

Lochlann had not been home to Drumshee for almost two years now. He was a great favourite with Brian Boru, the High King of Ireland. His father, Oscar, came to see him every few months and brought him news of home, but Lochlann never asked to return with him, even for a short visit. There was always some reason why he should not leave Kincora at that moment. Even when he formed part of the expedition to Kilfenora to demand the tribute of a hundred cows due to Brian Boru he still did not go the extra four miles to see his mother and his sister.

From time to time, Lochlann felt a pang of guilt. I should go back and see my mother, he thought. She had become blind just before he left home permanently when he was fourteen years old and he could not bear to see the change that had been made in her. She had been a bright, cheerful, competent woman helping on the farm, while his father worked his blacksmith business. And then one day, just the very day that Lochlann had arrived home for his summer holiday from the monastic school, she had gone into the forge and bent over the fire. A piece of iron-bearing sandstone had split and the hot iron ore had spurted out and burned her face. Her eye was so badly damaged that no sight was left. A few weeks later the sight began to leave the other eye. Soon she was completely blind.

The change in her was terrible. For weeks she wept hopelessly. Then she turned sour and bitter. Then she clung to her husband and her two children and demanded that someone was with her all of the time. He had been glad to leave. He had been glad of the excuse that his grandfather Ivar had wished that

Lochlann, his grandson, who had shared his blond hair and blue eyes as well as his Viking blood, should serve Brian Boru as soon as his fourteenth birthday arrived.

His sister, Nessa, was left behind. Whenever he thought of her, he felt uneasy. He knew that she bore the heavy burden of looking after their mother, of trying to keep cheerful, of fetching and carrying and of bearing with her mother's moods and doing the work that previously both she and her mother would have shared. Nessa would have loved to come to Brian Boru's court at Kincora. She would have loved the Great Hall with its painted leather hangings, and the *Grianán,* or Sunroom, where the ladies of the court spent their time singing, and stitching embroidered cloths, but someone had to stay at home.

'My mother wishes my sister to stay at Drumshee with her,' he said abruptly.

'That is sad about your mother,' said the queen softly.

She has her father's interest in people, thought Lochlann. Not many queens would be interested to hear the family news of a messenger.

'You must not let your sister sacrifice herself, though,' she continued. 'She has her own life to lead. Once this battle at Dublin is over you must see to it. Perhaps some woman living locally could care for

14

your mother and then your sister could go to Kincora. I'm sure my father would welcome her.'

Lochlann bowed. He did not want to think about his mother, or about Nessa now. He was fired with a passionate longing to be on his way and to bring the good news to Brian Boru that Malcolm II of Scotland was sending aid to him.

The queen, however, still lingered. 'Whom does your sister look like?' she asked. 'Does she look like her grandmother, Emer, with her dark blue eyes and her dark curly hair, or is she blond like her grandfather?'

'She looks like me, I think,' said Lochlann hesitantly. It was a strange thing, but he could hardly recall Nessa's face. After the years at the monastic school and then the time at the court of Brian Boru, he had almost forgotten what his sister looked like.

'I must give you a present for her,' said the queen. She put her two hands to the shoulder of her cloak and touched a magnificent brooch, made from gold and studded with rubies. Carefully she opened the pin and held it out.

'Give this brooch to your sister. Tell her it's a gift from me in memory of her grandmother. Wait, I will write to her. It was your grandmother who taught me to write.' She went over to the table at the side of the room, took a small piece of vellum, dipped the quill in the inkhorn and wrote a few words. Then she looked up and looked closely at him. She smiled, bent her head, and then wrote another few words. Then she dusted the ink with some sand and when it was dry she carefully wrapped the brooch in the vellum and sealed the little parcel with some red wax.

Lochlann took the small package and stored it carefully within his pouch.

'I've written to your sister and told her what I think she should do. I've told her that you are so like your grandfather and that yet, there is one thing about you that reminds me of your grandmother,' she said, looking at his fair-skinned young face. 'You bring back happy memories of my days at Kincora. Now don't forget to give this to your sister.'

'I will go to see her and give her this as soon as the battle in Dublin has been won,' he promised with a smile, and she smiled back. The young are full of courage, she thought. No foreboding of the future ever disturbs their minds. Would the battle really be won? Would her father, Brian Boru, survive? And what about her brothers Murrough, Flann, Teige, Donogh, her nephews, and this silver-haired, blue-eyed boy, grandson of her beloved tutor, Emer? Would they all survive?

'Safe home,' she said softly.

Chapter 2

The way home did not seem long to Lochlann, though it took two days to ride from King Malcolm's palace at Dunkeld, in the centre of Scotland, back to Strathclyde on the east coast. Scotland was a difficult country to cross, full of mountains, but Donal of Knockbrack, whom Brian Boru had sent with him, knew the way well and he led Lochlann through the valleys and along the great rivers that ran like seams through the valleys.

'Look there are Malcolm's galleys, down there in the Firth of Clyde,' said Donal. Lochlann looked down at the great ships, each one of them capable of holding a hundred men.

'One of them will soon be on its way to Limerick,' he said with satisfaction. 'It will be a great battle, Donal, and perhaps we'll end the power of the Vikings in Ireland for ever and Brian Boru, and after him his son Murrough, will rule over a peaceful and united Ireland.'

'With the help of God,' said Donal piously. 'Only a few more miles to go now to Lunderston Bay and we'll find our own ship waiting for us.'

The small galley was where they had left it, tucked into a cove. Donal had left a full shipload of men on board, while he and Lochlann made their way across Scotland and back. Viking pirates frequently ravaged that coastline and would take over any unprotected ship they could find.

Swiftly they sailed back down the Scottish coast passing Bute and Arran on their right and reaching the coast of Donegal by dawn. Lochlann drew in a deep sigh of relief. He knew that there still was danger from Viking pirates even on the west coast of Ireland. Nevertheless he felt at ease to be back within sight of his own country so he lay down on the deck, rolled himself in his heavy fur-lined cloak and fell asleep.

In two days' time, with this strong north wind behind us, we will sail up the River Shannon and then we will march to Dublin for the great battle. This was his last thought before his eyelids fell heavily over his exhausted eyes.

The galley was in sight of Sligo by morning. Then it sailed down past the coast of Mayo and was sailing past Galway by midnight. By the time that the galley sailed up the Shannon early the next morning, Lochlann was wide-awake and standing at the prow of the little ship. The galley passed Limerick, its docks busy and active. In the time of Lochlann's grandfather, Ivar, this had been a Viking settlement, but now Brian Boru had conquered it. There were still many Viking traders working there, but they all paid tribute to Brian Boru and were under his rule.

The ship did not stop at Limerick but at Kincora, a few miles outside Limerick, just where the mighty river of the Shannon flowed out from Lough Derg. The settlement was full of men-at-arms, noticed Lochlann. There were tents everywhere in the fields around the fort. Everywhere there were men-at-arms, shouting and calling to each other. He recognised some the tongues as he walked up from the riverside. The men from Donegal in the north were there; that was sure. He could hear also the lilting speech of the men from Cork in the south. Everyone was rallying to the call from the high king. And now he could bring good news: Malcolm of Scotland would send two hundred and fifty men.

Quickly he strode through the gates nodding to the guard and making his way to the Great Hall, which had been built inside the fort of Kincora.

'Wait,' said a guard as he approached. 'The king is talking with his son. Murrough is in with him.'

And indeed everyone around knew this, as the sounds of two mighty voices rose and swelled in the still air.

'Why do you have to come?' shouted Murrough. 'You are seventy-six years old. Why can't you leave the fighting to me? Why can't you stay at home as old men do? Stay at home and say your prayers. Pray for victory. That's all you can do at your age!'

Listening outside, Lochlann suddenly felt cold. If Brian Boru were to stay back from the battle, then his bodyguard would have to stay at Kincora with him.

'Fool!' came the impassioned voice of the old king. 'Don't you know why the men fight? They fight for me! They fight because I am there at their head. They fight because they know that I ask nothing of them that I do not ask of myself. I am going to Clontarf. Nothing that you can say will stop me going.'

'You can't go,' shouted Murrough. 'You have made me commander of the army. My word goes. I say that you stay at home.'

There was a sudden silence. Lochlann clenched his hands. It was true. Murrough was the commander of the army. Brian Boru, himself, had invested his son with the supreme command. What would he do now? What could he say? Everyone around held his breath. Lochlann noticed his old enemy, Turlough, son of

Murrough, listening nearby. Turlough, like himself, was part of Brian Boru's bodyguard. If his father, Murrough, got his way, Turlough, also, would have to stay at Kincora to guard the king, his grandfather, while others marched to Clontarf and to a glorious victory.

'I'll tell you what I'll do,' said Brian Boru's voice. This time it was no longer hard and angry, but held all the charm of a man who always knew how to get his own way. 'I'll go with you to Clontarf – no, let me finish – I'll go with you to Clontarf, I'll talk to the men before the battle. I'll tell them what they are fighting for. I'll inspire them with my vision of a united Ireland and then before the fighting starts, I'll retire to my tent. Do you agree to that, my son, the commander?'

'I agree,' said Murrough levelly. He had obviously decided to ignore the mocking note in the last sentence. 'I agree to that as long as you keep at least one bodyguard with you. Then he can summon help if needs be.'

'I'll keep Lochlann,' said the old king. 'He will stay with me for his grandfather's sake.'

Outside Lochlann looked at Turlough and then looked away. He could not bear the look of triumph on his enemy's face. Turlough was a few months

younger than he; Turlough was still only fifteen years old, but he would be out there fighting while Lochlann stayed behind as nursemaid to an old man.

Suddenly the door was flung open and Brian Boru strode out followed by Murrough.

The room outside the king's chamber was crowded with chieftains and kings from all over Ireland, but King Brian ignored them all.

'Lochlann,' he said clapping his sinewy old hand on the boy's shoulder, 'they told me you had arrived. Come and sit by me at dinner. You can tell me the news from Scotland and what said my son-in-law, Malcolm.'

So Lochlann proudly followed the king into the Feasting Hall, and proudly took his place at the king's own high table, which stood on a platform overlooking the other tables and facing the door.

There was a firepit in the centre of the floor, but that was for heat only; all the food was cooked in the kitchen – a separate building, but joined to the Feasting Hall by two long passages. Along one passageway came roasted haunches of venison, steaming silver dishes with woodcock and quails laid out on them, succulent sausages and puddings, baskets of bread, platters of vegetables, while down the other passageway would go the dirty plates and the remains of the food. A hundred candles of beeswax burned on the tables and in the corner an old man strummed gently on a harp.

'Tell me of Malcolm,' said the king again and looking down at the lower tables, Lochlann caught Turlough's envious eye and smiled teasingly at him, before deferentially bowing his head to the king and recounting his mission to Scotland.

It was almost midnight by the time that Lochlann staggered sleepily out from the Feasting Hall. He stood for a moment resting his aching head against the smooth wood of the doorpost. He was intoxicated not so much by the ale that he had drunk, as from the talk that he had listened to between King Brian and his son Murrough. He had told his tale of Malcolm. They had laughed at his words – two great men congratulating him. Then they had spoken of the battle to come – one on either side of him – and they had discussed their manoeuvres.

'The Vikings will come in from the sea,' said Murrough. 'If we can arrive at Dublin before they do, it will be a five-day march through Thomond, Ossary and Meath. But if we can get ahead of them, we can meet them on the bank and turn them back.'

'No,' said Brian. 'We will lose too many men like

that. The Vikings are better with the bow and arrows than our men. Let them come ashore and then fight them face to face, hand to hand.'

'Where will we set up our camp then?' asked Murrough.

'There's a hillside just above where the River Tolka enters the sea,' said Brian. 'The place is called Clontarf. We can set up camp there.'

And Lochlann smiled to himself as he thought of how he had broken in to the conversation, almost as though he were an equal of two such powerful men.

'We'll have to make sure that the Vikings from the sea – Brodar of the Isle of Man and Sigurd of the Orkneys – can't join Sitric, King of Dublin,' he said eagerly.

Brian Boru, Emperor of the Irish, had clapped him on the shoulder. 'Well said, we'll put a strong force on the southside of the River Tolka to make sure that they can't get on to the Liffey and sail up to Dublin pool. Murrough, put your best archers there.'

And Murrough, Murrough the Tániste, the named successor to his father, Murrough the Proud, Murrough the Impatient, had nodded his head and even smiled at Lochlann.

Now at the thought of it, Lochlann slapped the doorpost with exultation flowing like mead through his veins. And at that moment Turlough hit him.

He must have been lurking in the shadows waiting. He hit Lochlann with a fist like iron and Lochlann dropped to the ground. He was up in a moment though, and in silence the two of them were locked together in battle. Every ounce of rivalry and jealousy came out in those blows and neither heard the voices of men returning to their lodgings after the feast. They had moved into the shadows beyond the Feasting Hall and were now behind the kitchen house. It seemed as if there would be no end to this fight. They were evenly matched in height and weight and neither wanted to give in. For over ten minutes they fought on grimly.

And then the high shrill cry of a banshee echoed around the fort. There was a shocked silence. All the shouts, the snatches of song and the roars of laughter ceased abruptly. The whole camp was quiet for a few minutes and then came a buzz of conversation. To hear a banshee on the eve of battle, that was an evil omen, indeed.

Both boys stopped fighting, their arms fell to their sides, and they stood frozen with dread. They stared at each other uncertainly. Turlough was the first to recover.

'That's for you, Yellow Hair,' he grunted. 'She is

crying your destiny. You are doomed to die at Clontarf.

And Lochlann stared at him, his throat and mouth gone suddenly dry, and he could think of no word to say in reply.

In the wail of the banshee, he had heard a name!

Chapter 3

Isle of Man 1014

The old woman bent over the fire. Harald watched her. The young Viking's nerves were on edge. He felt like screaming. Why didn't his mother come herself? Why had she asked him to do this? He hated it. He hated the small stinking room, the heat of the fire, the feeling of being caged. For the last six years his home had been the ship, his life the life of a pirate. He was the son of Brodar, the Norseman, hated by Saxon and Gael. He was a man, and a man to be feared. He hardly knew his mother, and now she had sent him on this fool's errand.

'Give me my answer and let me go,' he growled.

The old woman glanced up at him. He was as tall and as broad as a fully-grown man. She remembered when Brodar had first come to the Isle of Man and had seen Ingrid. That would be seventeen years ago on midsummer's day. This boy must be just sixteen. She had been present at his birth. She had given Ingrid the herbs that helped to deliver her of a fine man-child. And Brodar? The old woman snorted with disgust. He went back to the sea again immediately. Ingrid did not seen him for ten years. Then he arrived one day unexpectedly, just strolled into the house. Ingrid had been out, but ten-year-old Harald, who had been left to stir the slowly simmering pot over the fire, turned around, and instantly punched his father in the jaw.

'Like one of the hounds of Valhalla!' Brodar had recounted proudly to all his fellow pirates afterwards. Suddenly all the pride of fatherhood awoke in him. This strong, handsome, fearless boy was his son and Brodar was determined to have him. He stayed only three days on the Isle of Man – just long enough to father another child, and then he was gone, taking Harald with him. And now he was back again after six years and with him was Harald, grown out of all recognition.

The old woman gazed curiously at him. He was Ingrid's son; that was sure. He had her blue eyes, her fair skin and her yellow hair. He had his father's height and breadth of shoulder – a fine boy – a boy to be proud of. She shivered and looked into the fire again.

'You do not ask for yourself?' she murmured.

'How do you know I'm going, too?' he retorted.

She smiled. Of course, he was going. Sitric of

Dublin had asked for help against the threat of Brian Boru. If Brodar went, Brodar's son would go too. Then she frowned. Did she know his fate? A wisp of smoke blew out from the fire blurring the pictures there. His father's fate was clear. She could see it there amidst the smouldering peats. But the boy's? What was the boy's fate?

'Hand me the rowan twigs,' she said.

He reached out and then stopped. The rowan tree held a deep magic within it. It was dangerous to touch a rowan. He knew that.

'Get them yourself,' he said arrogantly, but his voice shook with fear. He turned his face away so that he could not see the laughter in her eyes. She stood up and took the small bundle of rowan twigs. She threw them on the fire. They flamed up, first blue, and then a clear searing yellow. She stared at them, her face still puzzled and intent. Then she passed her hand over her eyes, shook herself as a dog does when coming out of the sea, and then stood up.

'Your father will die in the battle at Dublin,' she said flatly. 'He will die at a place called Clontarf. Tell your mother that. Tell her to keep him here on the Isle of Man and he will avoid his fate. Or else he can take to the high seas and go where he wills. Tell him to go to Iceland, to Norway, to Orkney, but never to

Ireland. His death lies in Dublin, and only in Dublin. I see him dead there on the hillside above the sea, above Clontarf.'

Harald stared at her. He did not want to believe her.

'Old witch,' he muttered under his breath. It was useless saying the words; he knew that. No matter what he said, he did believe her. From right back to his early childhood that belief was ingrained in him. Everyone on the Isle of Man believed her. She had always been proved right. He kept his eyes on hers; trying to look for any shadow of doubt, any shadow of insincerity, but there was none. His gaze seemed to be locked in hers and he could not move.

'And now for your fate,' she said. She hesitated, sat down again and then stirred the fire. One of the peats in the fire collapsed with a puff of orange smoke. A strong pungent smell filled the little room. The old woman stared into the fire and then rubbed her eyes.

Suddenly Harald could stand the tension no longer. He backed away grasping with his hand for the rough wood of the door and then the cold iron of the latch. With one swift movement he clicked it open, slid out, and then slammed the door behind him.

A moment later he heard the click of the latch again. She had followed him out. Against his will, his head turned. She was standing on the doorstep looking after him. He stopped. It was as if his legs suddenly failed him. Her voice followed him.

'What about your own fate, Harald, son of Brodar?' she said softly.

And then he started to run. But as he ran he could hear, from behind, the sound of her laughter. There was a jeering and triumphant note in it and, oddly, it steadied him. He stopped running and pushed his yellow hair back behind his shoulders. 'Old witch,' he said again, but this time he said it with conviction and scorn. He knew what he was going to do.

The old woman gazed after him, shook her head and went back to her fire. She stared into it intently. Should she have persisted? Should she have tried to warn him? Could she have warned him? Can anyone warn a man against himself? She stirred the fire, but the same two mirror images remained.

★ ★ ★

'What did she say, Harald?' asked Ingrid as he came through the door of the small house where he had been born and where he had spent the first ten years of his life.

'She said that it will be a mighty battle and we will win a great victory and we will bring back gold and silver necklaces and bracelets and salted beef for the pot,' he answered fluently. His blue eyes shone and his white teeth flashed in a dazzling smile. He believed the words himself as he said them. He was looking forward to this battle. The life on the sea was good, but there were times when it sickened him. Some of these boats that they raided were too-easy prey – filled with merchants who could not fight and who died in terrible screaming states of fear. He was a man now and he wanted to meet great warriors. He wanted to fight in great battles. He wanted great songs to be sung about him. A battle would be great, he thought.

'What did I tell you!' shouted Brodar exultantly. 'I knew it. I felt it in my bones. Come on, boy; let's go down to the seafront. We'll check on the boats.

Without a glance at his wife, who was sitting by the fire cuddling Harald's six-year-old sister, Estrid, Brodar flung his arm over his son's shoulders and pushed him out of the door. Harald looked around the small settlement of twenty long low houses, their walls made from woven twigs of willow and alder and their roofs thatched with reeds. How stifling it all appeared to him now. He couldn't wait to get away from it. He couldn't wait to get out to sea again and to fight in a battle.

'Race you to the sea,' said Brodar and together they ran exuberantly down the thyme-scented turf until they reached the cliff.

Brodar's fleet of boats were there. All were the same: long boats with the dragon's head on the sharply pointed prow. The huge striped sails – sails that drove terror into the minds of all that saw them – hung from the top of each tall mast right down to the middle of each boat.

'How many ships will we take?' asked Harald.

'Three,' said Brodar. 'That should be enough. I'll leave a few here in case Malcolm of Scotland gets any ideas of attacking the Isle of Man while I am over in Ireland.'

Harald nodded. Three ships would give them a fighting force of two hundred-and-forty battle-hardened men. That would be a valuable aid to any king.

'What's it all about, Father?' he asked carelessly. Battles were battles. It didn't really matter what it was all about, but he was enjoying standing there in the late spring sunshine with his father's arm thrown across his shoulders.

'Well, I think two Irish kings – The High King Brian Boru and King Malachy of Tara – have been quarrelling with the King of Leinster. Sitric, King of Dublin, is supporting the King of Leinster, and we are coming to support Sitric and so is Sigurd from the Orkney Islands.'

A black cat suddenly started up from out of the bushes in front of them. Her tail was arched and her fur was fluffed out. Harald stared at her in dismay. Normally he took little notice of the superstition that a black cat crossing one's path brings bad luck, but now, just after the old woman's prophecy, he was suddenly afraid. He glanced at his father quickly, but the beaming smile had not faded and the blue eyes were still confident and excited.

'We'll leave at dawn,' said Brodar. 'We'll be in Dublin by tonight.'

* * *

Dawn was still just a grey mist and the air was clear and cold when they left the small, peat-smelling house. When they reached the boats the rowers were already on their benches, most of them stripped to the waist.

Brodar and Harald jumped into the lead boat, then the drummer began the rhythmic strumming, and the oars rose and fell in strict time to the beat. Once they were out in the open sea and the stiff northeasterly wind lifted the hair on the back of their necks, the sails were hoisted and the rowers sat back on their benches.

'It's Thor's blessing on us – a good wind,' shouted Brodar and all of the men laughed and cheered. Now the drummer took up another beat and the men sang the great saga of Beowulf and how he defeated his enemies. The ship plunged down the hollows in the sea and breasted up like a swimmer parting the waves. Its sharp keel seemed to cut through the water. Harald stood beside his father by the dragon prow and looked across the white surge of the waves. His eyes were young and keen and he was the first one on the ship to see the green smudge of land in the far distance.

'It's Ireland,' he shouted.

Just as the words left his mouth there was a harsh caw from overhead. A huge black raven shot through the blue sky and landed on the mast just over Harald's head. There was a sudden silence. The drummer missed his beat and the sound of men's singing died away. The raven was one of the god Odin's birds – the battle bringer. It was bad luck to see a raven on the eve of a battle. Harald looked up and saw the raven's cold grey eye fixed on him. He shivered, even though a moment before he had felt warm and confident. He stayed there staring at the raven and it seemed to him as if all the men on the boat were looking at him. Suddenly Harald heard words so clearly that he looked around to see whether anyone else had heard them also.

'What about your own fate, Harald, son of Brodar?'

Chapter 4

Holy Thursday of Easter, 1014

It was a clear fine day, well before nightfall, as the three long boats approached Dublin Bay. The city was on the southside of the inlet, or pool, from which it took its name (*Dubh Linn*, 'Black Pool). On fire with excitement, Harald leaned over the side of the long ship, resting his hand on his father's shield, which hung over the side of the ship.

'Look, there are the walls of Dublin, just on your left,' said Brodar from behind him. He leaned over the side of the boat and narrowed his long-sighted blue eyes. He snorted with disgust. 'Look,' he said, 'there's Sitric Silkbeard up there on the top of the ramparts and there's his mother with him. She's the sister of the King of Leinster – a woman that has caused lots of trouble! And that's Sitric's wife; she's a daughter of Brian Boru. The High King thought he could make friends with Sitric by that marriage,' he added, but Harald wasn't listening. All this talk of relationships and alliances and marriages bored him. He leaned over the side, shoulder to shoulder with his father. Now he could see the walls, fine strong walls, just beyond the pool, and inside them the Viking town of Dublin with its houses made from hazel wattle and plastered with mud.

'Are we going to land there by the walls?' Harald asked. His father shook his head.

'No,' he said. 'Brian Boru's men are all covering the entrance to Dublin. They must have marched across Ireland. They've arrived before us. We'll land here where the river enters the sea. I've been here before. I came trading for slaves at Dublin market about eight years ago. I think that river is called the Tolka. We'll be able to cut through and go across the hillside at the back of Clontarf there – we'll go around the back of his troops and enter Dublin from the west.'

Harald looked up and saw the hillside and suddenly he felt his lips go cold with shock. He had managed to forget the old woman, but now her words rang as clearly as if she were by his side:

'Your father will die in the battle at Dublin,' she had said flatly. *'He will die at a place called Clontarf. Tell your mother that . . . tell him to go to Iceland, to Norway, to Orkney, but never to Ireland. His death lies in Dublin, and only in Dublin. I see him dead there on the hillside above the sea.'*

Harald turned to his father. Brodar was a harsh man with his enemies; with his own men he could be a bully; to his wife, he was cold and indifferent; but to Harald he was a hero, almost a god. Harald worshipped his father and he could not bear to think that something might happen to him. He would have to tell him the truth; he would have to tell him what the wise old woman had said. It was not too late. What did Sitric, King of Dublin, matter to Brodar? They could just turn the dragonhead prow round, and with a good west wind behind them they would be back in the Isle of Man by daybreak.

'Father . . .' he said hesitantly.

But at that very moment an arrow flew from an Irish archer and stuck fast in the side of the ship just where one overlapping board met the board above it. The watchman cried out in alarm.

'Leave it, you fool,' shouted Brodar as a young sailor tried to pull the arrow out. 'Leave it or there will be a hole. Pull hard for the shore,' he yelled at the two banks of oarsmen. 'Keep them covered,' he bawled to the archers. Obediently they raised their bows and the rowers dipped their oars in the water. The drummer set up an insistent rapid rhythm.

'Row, you sons of dogs, row!'

'There's Sigurd's ships over there where the river

joins the sea,' screamed Harald.

'Steer for there,' roared Brodar. 'Keep those arrows flying. Row! Row faster! There we are now, we're out of range.' The show of force was enough and the small party of Irish archers withdrew. Brodar shouted the command: 'Moor the boats.'

Eventually the tents were raised, the fires were lit, the cooking pots were unpacked and the smell of fish stew filled the air. The archers kept their bows at the ready and even the oarsmen ate with their food in the left hand and their naked sword in the right, Brodar patrolled the men, leaving Harald in the party guarding the boats by the shore. It was sunset before Harald saw his father again. Eagerly he grabbed the edge of his father's cloak and drew him aside.

'Father,' he began, 'Do you remember when Mother sent me . . .'

'Brodar, my friend,' came a rough hoarse voice.

'Sigurd!' greeted Brodar enthusiastically.

'I have a cask of ale, in my tent,' went on Sigurd. 'Come and share it with me.'

'I don't need asking twice,' shouted Brodar. He patted Harald on the back and walked off shoulder to shoulder with the Earl of Orkney into the dusk of a misty Irish evening.

So Harald saw no more of his father that night.

And the next morning, Good Friday for the Christians, the two opposing armies were drawn up, the Vikings with their backs to the sea and the Irish with their backs to the hillside above Clontarf.

And by then, it was too late for any warning.

★ ★ ★

It was a clear cold dawn on the morning of Good Friday in the year 1014. The Irish and the men sent by Malcolm of Scotland had completed the long march from Limerick to Dublin in only four days to arrive in Clontarf by Holy Thursday. Lochlann stood holding the head of King Brian Boru's stallion. The king had spoken to his troops. He had reminded them that they fought for themselves, for their families, for their clans, and for their country. And they had raised a great shout of 'Boru *Abú*!' and Lochlann had known that at this moment these men fought because of their love and trust in their king.

But now they were silent. And all the troops on the other side of the battlefield were silent, also. The moment had now come. The quiet was slightly eerie. It seemed impossible that over eight thousand men should be gathered there and yet the high-pitched chatter of an early swallow should sound so loud in the grey dawn.

And then suddenly all changed. With startling

speed the sun rose up from behind the curve of the sea. The sky cleared to a deep blue, the church bell of the abbey of St Mary sounded the summons to prayer, the 6.00 a.m. service of matins. As soon as the last echo from the bell died away, the orange and white banner with its three lions was hoisted high above Murrough's head as he stood with his sword raised. And then Murrough lowered his sword; the Irish troops flowed down the hillside towards the flat ground of Clontarf and the battle commenced.

Some of those Vikings down there might be related to me, thought Lochlann, looking down at a boy of about his own age, whose flowing yellow hair seemed to glow in the sunshine. If my grandfather Ivar had not been captured by my grandmother's brother Conn, if Ivar had not joined with Brian Boru and given him all his loyalty – if that had not happened then I, Lochlann, might have been down there among the Vikings with my back to the sea.

'Let's go back to the tent,' said Brian Boru, and obediently Lochlann turned the stallion's head around and began to lead him back towards Tomar Wood where the king's tent had been set up.

They went along together in silence but just as they reached the outskirts of the wood Brian Boru gave a heavy groan. 'I wish I could die out there with a sword in my hand and not as an old man in my bed?' he said.

The pain in the king's voice pierced through Lochlann. For a moment he did not know what to say, but then words came to him.

'Many a man can fight; my lord,' he said, 'but only one man in Ireland could do what you did today. Look at how you inspired them. Look,' he repeated and turned the horse's head around to face down towards the sea. Brian's Boru's clan, the Dalcassians, had taken an early lead and were hacking and thrusting at the Vikings, each man with a short-bladed sword in one hand and a javelin in the other. In front of the men waved the banner above Murrough's head, the three golden lions gleaming in the early morning sunshine.

And then a great shout burst from the throats of the Irish troops. The Vikings seemed to give ground. Step by step, it looked as if they were being driven back. It might not last, Lochlann knew that, but for the moment the old king's face looked proud and happy.

'Come, my lord,' he said. 'Let me get you into shelter. If you are safe; Ireland is safe.'

★ ★ ★

Turlough thought his heart would burst with excitement and yet, he knew that he was afraid. All day long he fought by his father's side. First the Irish dominated the fight and then the Vikings, led by the indomitable Brodar of the Isle of Man, regained their position. As the day wore on the fight got more and more deadly. The ground beneath their feet became slippery with the blood of the wounded and of the killed. Still Turlough fought on, all the time seeing from the corner of his eye the banner with its three lions waving above his head. The three lions, he thought, as his sword parried and struck almost automatically, the three lions: Brian Boru, Murrough and Turlough – grandfather, father and son. The thought gave him renewed energy. With a quick slash of his sword across an enemy's neck he killed a Viking ahead of him.

And then suddenly the banner was no longer there. A violent onslaught of Vikings from the Orkneys had driven deep into the Irish battle lines. The standard bearer was dead, so was Oscar of Drumshee, and Murrough, his father, was badly wounded. Turlough bent over his father. The blood was gushing out from a wound on his chest – already his tunic was soaked with it. He could not live long; Turlough knew that. Already his father's face was grey with approaching death and his eyes were beginning to cloud over. But Murrough gathered all his strength and looked into his son's anguished eyes and said in a fierce whisper: 'Fight on!'

And Turlough fought on. Every blow he struck was like a scream of agony, but part of his mind had closed down and the fighting became a release for sorrow. A strange state of exultation came over him and he felt as if he alone could beat the Viking army.

Like the waves of the sea, the battle lines flowed and ebbed, but, like an incoming tide, the Irish troops pressed strongly against the foe, and advanced step by step, pace by pace, until the Vikings were driven into the sea.

With a shout of triumph, the Irish followed them, each man marking down an alien as prey. Turlough scrambled through the seawater after a young Viking. For a moment he almost slipped and he dropped his javelin, but then he grabbed the boy's yellow hair with his left hand and drove his short sword deep into the body.

And at that moment a Viking arrow pierced Turlough's neck and he dropped like a stone into the water.

And the sun set on a victory for Brian Boru.

But his son, Murrough, was fatally injured and lay dying in a tent at the side of the battle lines.

And his grandson, Turlough, lay dead in the shallow water at Clontarf Weir, his hands entangled in the yellow hair of a Viking.

Chapter 5

Nessa walked down the wet fields at Drumshee. It was the week after Easter and already the pale yellow primroses studded the banks under the hedges and on either side of the riverbank, the marsh marigolds gleamed like small bronze chalices.

Nessa was thinking about her mother, Aoife – thinking with despair that nothing she did seemed to lift the woman from the black depression that lay over her night and day. Oscar, Aoife's husband, had joined the army of Brian Boru and had marched to Dublin a week ago – and of course, wherever Brian Boru had gone, Lochlann, her son would have gone also.

'They'll die both of them,' Aoife had wailed when Nessa had asked her to come for walk down by the river. 'Those Vikings will kill them. They will torture them. They are fiends in human forms and they worship strange gods.'

And when Nessa had gently taken her mother by the arm and tried to raise her to her feet suddenly she screamed and sank down onto the floor staring with sightless eyes at the smouldering peats in the fire. Nessa left her; it was usually better to leave her to herself when those fits of anguish came over the woman, so she went out alone to bring the ducks back for their supper in the farmyard. She had almost reached the river when she heard the sound of her mother's voice.

'Nessa!'

Nessa clenched her teeth. Her own name had become hateful to her. It had become a thin wailing sound as harsh as a crow's lonely voice from the hillside. With an impatient sigh she turned to go back to the house. Remember she is blind, she told herself for the millionth time in the last two years. Remember how dark and dreary the world must be for her. I wish my father were back home again, she thought. This battle with Sitric, King of Dublin, would not last long, hopefully, and then Oscar's cheerful loud presence would fill the quiet sad household and the forge would ring once more with the clang of iron against iron.

'Nessa!' Again came the wailing cry.

Nessa climbed slowly back up the hillside. She swung the gate to the fort open, slipped through, and then closed it carefully behind her. Her mother was standing outside the silent fireless forge, her sightless eyes turned towards Nessa, her scarred face rigid with the effort of listening.

'Nessa?' she said tentatively, and then her acute ear caught the sounds of Nessa's leather boots on the stone path and that awful whining despairing note was back in her voice again.

'Nessa!' she wailed. 'What are we going to do if your father gets killed in that battle up in Dublin? There will be no one to work the forge and what will we live on then, you and me?'

'Don't think like that, mother,' said Nessa hurriedly. 'Father has been away fighting for Brian Boru before and he has always come home safely.'

'Of course there is always Michael over at Lough Fergus,' went on her mother, giving no impression that she even heard Nessa. 'He could send young Fintan over, but then that might not be much use. Your father makes swords and shields; they only make pots and pans . . . shovels and spades . . .' suddenly her words tailed off into a storm of weeping.

'Don't, mother,' Nessa bent over her mother, stroking her hair and patting her as if she were the parent, not the child. She was more patient and loving than usual as she was conscious of a feeling of shame that for one moment she had been glad that her mother's blindness had prevented her from seeing

Nessa's cheeks blaze red at the mention of Fintan.

How was he? she thought suddenly. He had heeded the call for all able-bodied men to join Brian Boru's army and march to Dublin to drive the Vikings out of Ireland. He was no soldier, not like Lochlann her brother – not even like her father who, though he was a blacksmith, was also a seasoned fighter. Would Fintan come back alive?

'Hush,' said her mother suddenly. Her own sobs had ceased and her hand fumbled across Nessa's face and then clamped firmly over her daughter's mouth.

'Hush,' she said again. In the silence Nessa heard the cheerful twittering of the first swallows of summer and, then, the sound that her mother had heard. A party of horsemen were splashing through the ford, the river crossing-place, at the bottom of the hill.

'It's them, mother, it's them!' shouted Nessa struggling free of her mother's hand. 'Let me go, let me go and see! I'll come back straight away and tell you when I see that he is safe.' She said 'he' but she meant 'them'. To her shame, Fintan's safety was as important to her as that of her father and brother.

'No,' screamed her mother. 'Take me with you.'

Nessa clenched her teeth in fury. Left to herself she could have run swiftly out of the fort, down through the damp mossy fields, but, fitting her pace to her mother's faltering footsteps, they were barely at the gateway by the time that the party of horsemen had climbed the hill.

And one look at the riderless stallion told her what had happened.

Swiftly Fintan dismounted. With one quick glance at the scarred listening face of Aoife, he looked compassionately into Nessa's horror-stricken eyes and then nodded slightly. Nessa walked forward trying to control the weakness in her legs. Silently Fintan uncovered the head and Nessa gazed down solemnly into the dead face of her father, Oscar of Drumshee.

'Nessa!' came the endless, plaintive, querulous cry.

Not even now can I have a moment to mourn my father, thought Nessa. She turned and put her arm around her mother

'There's bad news, mother,' she said quietly.

'He's not dead!' whispered Aoife, her hands framing her blind eyes as if she wanted to force herself to see.

There was a terrible silence. Nessa tried to force herself to speak but she could only hold her mother's thin body in her arms and look intently at the small robin perched on the bare branches of the tree overhead. It seemed strange that the bird could continue to sing so merrily with so much misery just beneath him.

'I'm afraid that your husband died in the battle of Clontarf,' said Niall of Corcomroe, stepping forward bravely, but turning his eyes aside from the terribly scarred face of the blind woman.

Aoife threw herself down on the ground and the sound that came from her was like that from a banshee – a wild, wailing noise that raised the hair on the back of the necks of the men that stood around.

'Mother, don't!' said Nessa despairingly. I can't even mourn my dead father, she thought. Though she knew that she was being unfair, she was conscious of a feeling of anger beneath her misery.

'I'll take her in the house,' said Fintan, gently detaching the distraught woman from Nessa's arms and carrying her inside. Quickly Nessa straightened her back – everything depended on her now. Her father would no longer be around to take the burden occasionally from her shoulders.

'Bring my father's body in,' she said steadily 'I'll have to find some neighbours to dig the grave.'

No need for that,' said Niall gently. She was a beautiful girl, he thought. What a terrible thing for her to be immured here with that mad woman. 'My men will do all that, but first . . .' He glanced back at the second leather stretcher. Nessa's cornflower blue eyes widened with a sudden dread. He had not mentioned Lochlann, had not said: 'I'll send your brother home to be with you.'

For a moment she stared at Niall wordlessly, and when she spoke it was in the dead tones of one who expects nothing, hopes for nothing.

'He's dead, too,' she said, and there was no note of question in her voice.

'No, no,' said Fintan coming hastily to Nessa's side.

From the house behind them rose a wail from Aoife, but Fintan ignored it. Quickly he took Nessa's cold hands in his. His heart almost burst with pity for the lovely girl.

'No, Nessa,' he repeated earnestly. 'Lochlann is alive. He has been wounded in the leg and we think he has a fever, but that is all. Will we bring him in?'

Nessa stared at him in bewilderment. He took her in his arms. He did not care about Niall's curious glance, or for the men standing behind. Nessa leaned against him for a moment. He felt strong and dependable. Suddenly she felt his strength flow into her. She moved back, but she still kept her hand within Fintan's large warm one. She looked at Niall.

'If your men can dig the grave in the burial ground at Clogher . . .' she said. 'Will you . . .will you bury my father today? My mother is in no state to attend the burial and I cannot leave her. She can visit the grave afterwards when . . . when she is well again. But now I must care for my brother. Fintan will take you to Clogher after you take Lochlann into the house.'

'I'll be back later,' said Fintan in a low voice as he bent down to seize two of the handles of the leather stretcher. Nessa said nothing, but she felt a slight feeling of warmth tingle the tips of her fingers. It was a good feeling to know that she was not completely alone.

'Your brother's not too badly hurt, you know,' said Niall reassuringly. 'The healers said that he will soon recover. The wound on the leg is closing up well. He is young and strong. He will soon be up and about and helping you to care for your mother.'

Chapter 6

The boy inside the cottage opened his blue eyes. He had been sick and drowsy and wearied by the jolting swinging motion of the horses, but now he realised that he had been placed on a bed. He still felt dizzy, but he could now see more clearly. His eyes rested on the blackened timbers of the roof, the sooty thatch above them, then swung around to see the fire with the iron pot hung over it. The two seats beside the fire, the sheepskin on the floor, and the beds in the curtained-off sleeping places around the walls of the house – they all had a familiar air, and the sight of them soothed and settled him. He closed his eyes again, but the scenes of battle were still there. He could not shut them out. Clontarf – now it seemed to him a terrible word. The screams of dying men, the sickly smell of blood, news of small victories, terrible catastrophes, news came from all sides. Suddenly he sat up in bed. He was remembering now. Murrough, the son of the old King Brian – he was dead. That had been the first piece of news. And so was his sixteen-year-old son,

Turlough – that news had come towards the end of the battle. Sigurd of Orkney was dead, the messenger had related, and then, an hour later so was the King of Leinster. But all that news had come before the final terrible deed. The boy shuddered violently and an icy sweat drenched his blond hair. Then his head fell back. The bed was soft and the pillow of sheep's wool was stuffed with fragrant herbs. His golden eyelashes fell over his eyes and in a moment he had fallen back into that sick heavy sleep again.

When Nessa came back in, it looked as if he had not moved. She cast a quick glance at him and then went over to her mother.

'Try to sleep,' she whispered gently, lifting the woman's legs onto the bed and covering her with a blanket woven from the brown wool that came from their own sheep. The sight of that wool reminded her that she needed to check on the sheep down in the Isle of Maain. She would wait until Fintan came back, she decided. It would not be safe to leave either her mother or her brother for the moment. She would have to leave the ducks to fend for themselves down on the River Fergus, also. Hopefully, no foxes would get them once night fell.

In the meantime, she decided, she would dress the wound on her brother's leg; the long journey would have done it harm. She went to the wooden dresser and took down the jar of medicine made from the herb woundwort. It was running low, Nessa noticed. The abscess around her mother's injured eye had grown worse recently. Nessa had been using the medicine to treat it daily, but there was almost no improvement. I should get Old Bridget to look at her, she thought and then she sighed. There was little chance of her mother tolerating the presence of Bridget in the house, and certainly none of her allowing Bridget to examine the infected eye.

'Well, at least, Lochlann will soon be better and then we'll be able to tackle her together,' she said aloud as she folded back the bedcovers.

'Lochlann!' she exclaimed. The golden eyelashes lifted and there was a flash from the blue eyes. But then the eyes closed again and the boy seemed to sleep. 'Lochlann!' she exclaimed again. For a moment she could have sworn that she saw something in his eyes – not recognition – more like fear. But why should Lochlann fear his own sister? Nessa sighed again and with a steady hand peeled away the sodden linen wrappings, smeared the clean strips with the herbal paste and carefully bandaged the wound again. Niall of Corcomroe was right, she thought as she threw the old bandages on the fire and washed her hands with water from the wooden bucket that stood beside the door. Yes, she said to herself, the wound is definitely healing. The skin around it was pink, not the angry red which would have shown that the infection was spreading. She laid her hand on her brother's forehead. There was no fever, there. He would soon be well and then the burden of Aoife's illness and the care of the animals would be shared.

'Nessa,' the querulous voice had begun again. Aoife's periods of sleep were getting shorter and shorter. I wonder is she in pain, thought Nessa. Perhaps I might distract her with talk of Lochlann. She might come to her senses again if she knew that he was still alive and in need of her love. Carefully she replaced the bed covers over Lochlann and turned to her mother.

'Mother,' she said hesitantly 'Come over here with me. Give me your hand. There is someone here for you. Let me put your hand on his face – feel his face. It's Lochlann, mother. He's hurt, but he will soon be himself again. Don't pull away, mother. I tell you it is Lochlann.'

The effect of this simple request was complicated. Aoife allowed her hand to be placed on the boy's face. For a moment there was a look of intense yearning, but then she snatched her hand back. She said nothing, just stumbled back across the floor, feeling her way around the sharp corners of the table, and sat down by the fire. Nessa was so puzzled by her mother's strange behaviour that it was only later that she remembered that the boy on the bed had jerked convulsively when the woman's hand had touched his face.

'Mother,' she said sharply. 'It's Lochlann, your son Lochlann. Don't you want to help me to nurse him? Sit by him, Mother, talk to him. He will soon come to his senses when he hears you speak.'

'That's not Lochlann,' said Aoife. Her voice was low and it sounded more normal than usual.

'Of course it is Lochlann,' persisted Nessa. 'They've brought him back from the battle of Clontarf. He wasn't killed. He will soon be well again.'

'That's not Lochlann,' repeated Aoife. She did not turn her head but stared steadily, with her sightless eyes, into the depths of the smouldering peats on the fire.

Nessa shrugged. There was no point in arguing. Her mother grew worse every day. Now there were very few times left when her mind was clear. Nessa went to the door and stared down the misty fields. There was no sign of anyone coming. She went back into the house and sat beside the bed where Lochlann lay. Her mother seemed to have dropped off into one of her sudden dozes and after a few minutes Nessa herself closed her eyes – she had been up most of the previous night with her mother and she was exhausted. Soon she was fast asleep.

Two hours passed. The boy on the bed slept also. He slept and he dreamed. He dreamed of Clontarf. Now he was in the tent. There were four of them in that tent. Two men: one Viking, one Irish; and two boys: one Viking and one Irish. And the old man, King Brian Boru was dying. Blood flowed everywhere. There was a sickly sweet smell from it. The boy was already dead when King Brian suddenly snatched a sword and with unbelievable strength slashed the Viking man's legs. Both legs were severed at the thigh. The scream was terrible! It rang through the little tent and then it seemed to ring through the roof of the small house.

Nessa jumped to her feet. She was shaking all over. She bent over the bed and cradled the boy in her arms.

'Lochlann, Lochlann,' she cried. 'It's all right. You're all right. You're home. I will look after you.'

Quite suddenly the screaming ceased. The blue eyes opened for a moment and then closed again.

The boy turned his head away.

And then the door burst open.

'Nessa,' said Fintan. 'Are you all right? What's the matter? Who screamed like that?' His eyes went to the quiet figure of Aoife by the fireside. She had not moved. She had not turned her head, thought Nessa, and yet the scream had been loud enough for Fintan to hear as he came through the fort.

'It's all right, Fintan,' she said quietly. 'It was Lochlann. He had a nightmare, I think.'

'I'm not surprised,' said Fintan sombrely. 'I saw enough at Clontarf to give any man nightmares.' He sat on the end of the bed and held out his arms to her. She went to him and said nothing for a few minutes, feeling the strength of his arms around her and luxuriating in the feeling of being loved and being cared for.

'What happened at Clontarf?' she asked eventually. 'Was it a victory for the Vikings and for the King of Leinster?'

'No,' said Fintan. 'It was a great victory for us. But it was a victory that cost us dear. King Brian Boru had promised his son Murrough to stay out of the battle – he was seventy-six-years old, you know – and he stayed in his tent in Tomar's Wood beside the battlefield. Lochlann stayed with him. The battle was almost over and the Vikings were defeated, but Brodar from the Isle of Man, and his son, escaped. They must have been fleeing through the wood when they came upon the tent. No one knows what happened. But King Brian Boru was killed and so was Brodar's son. Brodar himself was terribly injured and he died soon afterwards. Lochlann was unconscious and had a wound in his leg.'

'And my father?' questioned Nessa in a low voice.

'Oscar was killed on the battlefield. He was fighting side by side with Murrough. First your father was cut down, and then Murrough. They were both killed.'

Tears welled up in Nessa's eyes, but she said no more. There was no more to be said. Oscar was dead and now she had to care for his still-living wife and his injured son. She looked across at her mother and sighed – Aoife was the greatest problem. Lochlann would recover. He already showed signs of coming out of his unconscious state. But her mother . . . Fintan followed the direction of her eyes.

'Nessa,' he questioned. 'What is wrong with your mother? I know that she is blind and I know that she is depressed. But she seems different now, different to how she was before I went away to battle . . . she seems . . .'

'Almost mad,' finished Nessa in as steady a voice as she could command. 'I know.'

'I'll go and get Old Bridget,' said Fintan decisively, rising to his feet and putting Nessa gently on the ground. 'No, don't argue,' he said putting a finger on Nessa's lips. 'Let me get her. At least she can look at Lochlann and with luck she will be able to examine your mother.'

And then he was gone. Nessa sat back again on the bed. Fintan would not be long. Old Bridget lived in a little cottage down near the flat land by the bog at the Isle of Maain. She looked across at her mother. The woman was soundly asleep. If she could stay asleep while Bridget looked at her, all might pass without those screams of hate which Nessa so dreaded.

All was still quiet when Fintan arrived back with Bridget. Nessa had not heard him arrive; he must have left his horse outside the gate to the fort, and the small fat woman, smelling strongly of herbs, was inside the door before she had realised that anyone was there. Quickly she put her finger to her lips and the old woman nodded. She stood just inside the door, with Fintan hovering behind her, and looked across at Aoife, still sleeping soundly by the fireside. She looked at her for a long time, opening the door as widely as she could so that the light from the setting sun could stream in through the west-facing door. Then she nodded and turned towards the bed where Lochlann lay. Nessa drew back the bed-coverings and unwound the strips of linen from his leg. The wound seemed even better than when she had dressed it a few hours ago, she thought. The skin just next to the wound had now turned from red to pink. Bridget touched it gently, feeling the firm young flesh, and then nodded with satisfaction. She took a clay jar from her pouch and scraped out some green paste and put it on the linen strips and then quickly and expertly tied them again. Nessa replaced the bed coverings, conscious that Bridget had turned away and was now standing close to Aoife.

'Talk to your mother while Bridget looks at that eye,' whispered Fintan in Nessa's ear and Nessa stood beside Bridget and with as steady a voice as she could muster said:

'I'll just put some more ointment on your eye, mother.'

For a moment it seemed to be working. Aoife continued to keep her face turned towards the fire and her expression was indifferent, but something, perhaps a different smell, struck her. Frantically she groped around and her hand touched Bridget's cloak and she began to scream:

'Thieves! Murderers! Oscar, Oscar, get them out of here. Help! They are trying to murder me!'

Quickly Bridget smoothed some more of the ointment from her jar over the abscess around Aoife's eye and then slipped out of the cottage and closed the door behind her.

'There is no one here in the house except me and Fintan, mother,' said Nessa bravely. 'Try to sleep now. You have been having bad dreams.'

A blank look spread over Aoife's face. Her head fell heavily forward and her breathing became slow and quiet. She had fallen asleep again. With a few backward glances, Nessa tiptoed to the door and Fintan followed her. Bridget was standing quietly outside.

'I'll give you this for the lad,' she said handing Nessa the jar of green paste. 'That's goosegrass – great for healing wounds. He will do well. There is no fever. I can't understand why he is not awake.'

'It might be that he just needs some time' said Fintan. 'He must have seen some terrible things. He was there when the king was killed.'

'That could be it,' said Bridget thoughtfully. 'Anyway, he will recover soon. Feed him some soup and some warm milk.'

'And my mother?' asked Nessa bravely, clenching

her hands so tightly that her nails dug into the palms.

Bridget's face changed. 'Not good,' she said shortly. 'I'll have to think. There's something badly wrong there. It's outside my knowledge. Could you get a healer to come and see her? They have a man at Kincora, someone was telling me. The king brought him there from across the sea and he has great knowledge.'

'I'll ride over,' said Fintan eagerly. 'I'll be back in a day. I'll start sometime tomorrow morning.'

Bridget nodded. 'Yes, do that, the sooner the better.' She hesitated and then went on, 'I think it's not just a matter of the eyes, and of that sore where she was burned. The sore should have healed over long ago. I'm wondering whether there is some way that the infection could have got into the brain. I don't know, but that's what I am thinking.'

And that's what I have feared, thought Nessa.

'But will you be all right here on your own, Nessa?' asked Fintan suddenly doubtful.

'She's managed before; she can manage for another few days,' said Bridget briskly. 'The sooner someone who has the knowledge looks at that eye, the better it will be for all of them.'

Nessa took a deep breath. She smiled at Fintan. 'Go and may God go with you,' she said.

Chapter 7

'I hate soup!' said Nessa aloud. Depressed by the silence of the house, she had begun to talk to herself. Her mother showed no reaction, but Lochlann turned his head for a second. Nessa watched him.

'Lochlann,' she said, but there was no response. His eyes were still tightly closed. Perhaps she had only imagined that he had turned. Perhaps she had only imagined a flash of blue from under the eyelids. Despondently, she went back to cutting up the vegetable roots with her sharp knife. She would boil them up for soup. There was no use cooking anything other than soup these days. Both her mother and her brother had to be cared for and fed as if they were babies. Her mother took very little – she had begun to lose weight at an alarming rate – but Lochlann gulped down the liquid hungrily. He never opened his eyes, though, and Nessa had begun to despair.

'And yet the wound is clean and is healing,' she said to the knife, holding it up so that she could see her blue eyes and blond hair in its shiny surface. Everyday when she dressed his wound, it looked a little better. Perhaps, he too, like her mother was injured in the brain. She sighed, put the root vegetables into the iron pot which hung over the fire, threw in a few handfuls of sorrel pulled fresh from the hedge by the lane, put the knife back beside the bread basket, and then crossed the room and looked out of the door.

'Where is Fintan?' she tried saying to a startled duck that scuttled past. And then she sighed once more. Fintan had been gone for three days now. Of course, he would have to wait for the healer and there were probably many wounded warriors at Kincora. They would have to be seen to before the healer could come here. At the back of her mind she had a niggling fear that the healer might not come, at all. It would not seem important to come forty miles to see a woman with an abscess around her eye.

'I'll just walk down to the ford,' she said snatching her cloak from the iron nail behind the door. She felt as if she could not bear to stay in that silent house one minute longer. The air outside was fresh and clean and the tight white buds on the hawthorn trees were just beginning to burst open

'Tomorrow will be the first of May,' she said sadly.

Last year she and Fintan had wandered the fields hand in hand and Fintan had told her that he loved her and that they would be married next spring. And now she was alone with a sick brother and a sick mother to look after and perhaps Fintan would stay at Kincora and would never come back again. And yet, as she went down the steep fields towards the crossing-place on the River Fergus, she kept expecting to see his horse at any moment.

'I'd better go home,' she muttered after five minutes of standing, and looking, and listening. 'He won't come tonight. It's getting too late.'

The small house within the fort seemed darker than ever. On the chair by the fire sat her mother, twitching from time to time, and on the bed lay Lochlann, sleeping soundly. Nessa bent over him. His breaths came slowly and steadily. Sometimes, she imagined, he was not really asleep, but was just lying there with his eyes closed, but now he seemed to be in a true, deep sleep. She sat on the chair on the opposite side of the fire to her mother and closed her own eyes. But it was no good. She could not sleep. She felt restless and unable to settle. She got up and started to move around the room, straightening iron mugs and platters on the dresser and tidying away things from the floor.

In the corner behind the bed there was a pile of Lochlann's clothing. When Niall and Fintan brought him in they had undressed him and left him in his linen undershirt. Nessa picked up the gold-embroidered *léine* (tunic) and the crimson *brat* (cloak). With a sudden pang she remembered her mother patiently stitching the *léine* and she herself had helped to weave the crimson *brat* from white wool dyed with the roots of madder. Lochlann had looked magnificent when he wound the folds of the *brat* around him and fastened it at the shoulder with a silver brooch purchased at Coad Fair.

I was so proud of him, thought Nessa. She sighed and then carefully she placed the two garments in a wooden chest, and then bent down to pick up the leather pouch. She opened it. There was just one thing in it; a small packet sealed with wax. She broke the seal and a brooch rolled out – a magnificent brooch, made from gold and studded with rubies. Beside it was a small roll of fine vellum.

Nessa gazed at the brooch for a moment. Where had her brother got something like that? This was a brooch that a king might wear. Suddenly curious, she unrolled the vellum. It was a letter. Nessa turned it over and gazed at the signature at the back of the letter. It was from Bebhinn, Queen of Scotland. Of course, Bebhinn was one of Brian Boru's daughters; Nessa knew that. She had been sent to Scotland to marry Malcolm II, High King of Scotland. Nessa's grandfather Ivar had told her about that. He had been one of the party that formed her escort when she had left Ireland. Lochlann must have been sent to Scotland on a mission, thought Nessa, and the queen had given him the brooch as a keepsake.

But no, the letter was not addressed to Lochlann; the letter was for her. Nessa's eye found her own name. The brooch was for her, also, she realised, as she skimmed down through the words. She walked over to the table under the small window and folded back the shutters so that she could see properly. Her hands shook with excitement as she unrolled the vellum and held it open on the table.

Dear Nessa,

Your grandmother, Emer of Drumshee, taught me and my sisters and I send you this brooch in memory of the love that she gave to us, and of the love that we bore for her.

I wondered whether you looked like my beloved Emer, but your brother says that you are like him and so you must look like your grandfather, Ivar the Viking. You must be a very beautiful young girl. I have told your brother that he should take you to Kincora where you will meet many people and take part in the fun and festivities there. You must enjoy your youth! Your brother and your father should find someone to care for your mother so that your happiness is not sacrificed. I'm sure that my father, King Brian Boru, and my brothers would welcome you at Kincora. Bring this letter with you and show it when you arrive there.

Perhaps one day we will meet; but if not, remember that I send my fondest love for your health and happiness,

Bebhinn

Queen of Scotland.

Post Scriptum: I have just looked again at your brother and I see one thing on his face that reminds me of your grandmother. You may not remember her very well, but I do, and I remember she had a mole on her right cheekbone. 'My beauty spot', Emer used to call it. Your brother has the same mole in the same place and it made me homesick to see it.

Nessa read the letter twice over and then looked up, puzzled. Yes, she did remember now that Lochlann had a mole on his cheek. She had often teased him about it when they were both children. She used to shout: 'Lochlann you've got a piece of dirt on your cheek.' Funny, she thought, I never noticed the mole this time. She picked up a rushlight from the box at the side of the fireplace and carefully put the end of the wax in the fire. Then she crossed the room to stand before the bed where her brother lay. Slowly and cautiously she raised the rushlight. The boy lay there on the bed, blond hair spread out, blue-veined lids shut over blue eyes, dazzlingly fair skin – unmarked by any blemish or scar.

And there was no mole on this boy's face.

Suddenly Nessa knew the truth. Suddenly she knew that this was not Lochlann. At the back of her mind there had been doubts she realised that now. There had been something, perhaps more a lack of feeling than anything else, but there had been a puzzlement in her mind.

And her mother – of course, her blind mother had known that this boy was not Lochlann.

But if he were not Lochlann, who was he?

Suddenly she didn't want to know. She had relied so much on Lochlann coming to his senses, on Lochlann being once more a brother to her, on Lochlann taking some of the burden from her shoulders. Perhaps I'm mistaken, she thought. She looked over towards her mother. Aoife's eyes were open. She looked weary, but more peaceful than she had during the last few days. Nessa crossed the room and took her hand.

'Mother,' she said softly, 'come and see Lochlann.'

Slowly Aoife rose to her feet, clutching Nessa's

hand. Her blind face looked dazed and her hand burned into Nessa's. She has a high fever, thought Nessa, but I must know. Even though she is blind, surely her mother's instinct will tell her if this is her son. Carefully she supported her mother and urged her across the floor to stand beside the boy on the bed. She stretched down her mother's hand and placed it on the boy's face. 'Mother,' she said clearly and loudly into her mother's ear. 'This is Lochlann. Stroke his cheek.'

Some animation came into the blind woman's face. Her hand moved across the boy's forehead and down over his cheeks. She bent over him almost as if to kiss him. Nessa held her breath. Perhaps it was Lochlann.

But then Aoife suddenly drew back. She began to sob. 'That's not Lochlann,' she screamed. 'Why do you tell me lies? Why do you torment me? Where is Lochlann? Where is Oscar?'

Suddenly something snapped within Nessa. Her mother's sobs were almost too much for her to bear. She seized the boy's shoulder and shook him hard. 'Wake up,' she screamed. 'Wake up. Who are you? In God's name, who are you?'

The boy's blue eyes snapped open. There was no doubt about it. The eyes were sharp and intelligent.

They glanced with curiosity all around the little room and then rested on the terribly disfigured woman and the beautiful young girl. There was a look of calculation in those eyes and suddenly Nessa was afraid. He looked like Lochlann; that was true. What was it that the Queen of Scotland had said in her letter? '. . . like your grandfather, Ivar the Viking' that's what she had said. Lochlann had looked like a Viking. He had been named Lochlann – the old word for a foreigner – because of that. Desperately Nessa delved into her memory of her grandfather's lessons. She and Lochlann had both been taught to speak his native tongue.

'Who are you?' she asked in Norse.

The effect was terrible. There was no doubt, but that the boy understood. There was no doubt that he understood; no doubt that he knew that he had been discovered. His face went scarlet with anger and he sat up in bed and lunged towards her. His face was the face of someone who would commit murder from fear. He was not Lochlann, but a stranger. He was a Viking.

Quickly Nessa went over to her mother, seized her around the waist and dragged her across the floor and out through the door. She slammed the door behind them; the boy had a wound in his leg; even if he could drag himself across the floor he would not be able to follow fast enough to see where they were going.

For Nessa knew where she was going. In the centre of the Drumshee fort, right behind the forge, there was a secret hole. Down that hole there was a flight of stone steps that led to an underground room. This room had been a place of refuge in the past; Brian Boru himself had lain hidden there from the Vikings, her grandfather had told her. Now it was a place where she and her mother could hide from another Viking. They could stay there until Fintan got back from Kincora.

Chapter 8

Nessa carefully guided her mother down the stone steps to the underground room. It was cold and damp there, and quite dark. Just one faint glow of light from the setting sun streaked the wall at the top of the steps. The first thing to do would be to get a light, she thought, trying to keep her mind on ordinary everyday matters. Her mother was a dead weight on her. She had to drag her down from step to step.

'Where is that box, mother?' said Nessa bravely, endeavouring to keep her voice as unconcerned as possible. 'Do you remember the iron box that father made the summer you and I dipped all those rushlights?'

Aoife made no reply. I wonder does she remember anything, thought Nessa. Does she remember those hot summer days down in the river meadows, she cutting the rushes with a sharp sickle and me – two years younger than I am now – piling the sweet, scented rushes into the flat willow basket? That had been the enjoyable bit; peeling the rushes afterwards and taking care to leave just one green strip attached to the pith – that had been boring. But then the dipping of the rushes in the pot of warm liquid fat and hanging them up to dry – that had been fun, too. Nessa's eyes filled with tears. My life was so pleasant, and now it is so frightening, she thought.

Quickly she wiped the tears from her eyes with the back of her hand, forced open the lid of the box, and took out a rushlight. It felt stiff and solid in her hand. Good! The iron box had kept out the damp. She pulled out her knife and some tinder-dry moss from her pouch. Putting the moss on the ground, she struck her knife repeatedly on the flagstone until a small spark kindled a flame in the dried moss. As soon as the flame was steady, she thrust a rushlight into it, spilt a few drops of wax on the floor and anchored the rushlight safely to the wax. Quickly she rushed up the steps and pulled the flagstone across the hole. Now they would be safe. Even if the Viking boy came out of the house, he would see no sign of their hiding place.

The small room was now full of light and somehow it was comforting. Her mother was shivering, though. Aoife had hardly stirred from in front of the fire for the last few days. The damp cold of the underground room was too great a shock, too great a change for her. How can I keep her warm, thought Nessa.

'Mother,' she said aloud. 'Walk up and down with me. That will keep you warm.'

But Aoife crouched on the ground with her arms wrapped around herself, shivering violently, and no matter how hard Nessa tried she could not get her to move. Eventually she gave up and just sat beside her on the ground trying to warm her mother with the heat from her own body.

Hours passed and Nessa dropped into an uneasy doze. She had been awake most of the night before as her mother had been feverish and restless. As she slept she dreamed that the Queen of Scotland came to her and said: 'Your brother, Lochlann, is in that room over there. Go and find him.' Suddenly she woke with a start. Her dream was still very vivid and for a moment she thought that her dream was reality. Someone was saying the name 'Lochlann' over and over again. The voice was high and strange. Nessa shook her head to clear the fumes of sleep from her brain. This was her mother talking.

'Lochlann,' she was saying. 'Lochlann, don't go near the fire. Lochlann, you are only a baby. You are only two years old. Lochlann, you must keep away from the fire. Quick, Nessa, get the baby away from that fire.'

Nessa felt her face grow cold and damp with horror. This was terrible. Her mother was completely deranged. The fever had caused Aoife to lose the last of her wits. Her skin was burning to the touch and, by the light of the rushlight, her face looked grey, and her eyes were sunken.

Instantly Nessa made up her mind. If Aoife had to spend a night in this damp underground room she might die.

I'll have to get her back into the house, she thought. I need that fever drink that Bridget gave me for her. I need to get her into her warm bed by the fire. It was stupid to run away. I don't need to be scared of that boy. After all he is wounded. He is lame. I'll slip away now; she won't even notice that I have gone.

The moon was high in the sky above the river valley when Nessa came up from the underground room. She lifted the flagstone, stood at the top of the steps, and took a deep breath to give herself courage.

'He's only a boy,' she said aloud. 'And he is wounded in the leg. I can manage him.' In her hands she held a rope made from plaited leather. Her father used it for tying up difficult horses when he shoed them. If necessary she would tie this boy up, she planned. Whatever happened, she dare not leave her feverish mother any longer in that cold, damp underground room. Cautiously she crept around the corner of the forge. A soft glimmer of light shone through the cracks at the side of the door and the air smelled of that sharp acid smoky smell of smouldering peat. The fire must still be burning, then, she thought with surprise. She had been afraid that it would have burned itself out with no one to put new turfs of peat on it. For a moment she hesitated, but then she forced herself to go forward. She pushed open the door softly and then stepped inside. Her glance went immediately to the bed – Lochlann's bed – at the back of the little house.

There was no one there. The bedcoverings were thrown back and the bed was empty. The room was empty. The boy had gone. He must have dragged himself out of his bed and gone away. Perhaps he was out there in the darkness somewhere. Nessa did not allow herself to even think about that possibility. First she would get her mother back into the house and then she would slam the door, and drag over the table, and perhaps the wooden dresser also, and put them against the door. Even if the boy had only been pretending to sleep all those days, he was still weak and ill. He must have been; otherwise, he would have tried to escape long ago. Probably he knew a little of the Gaelic language so he understood that he had been mistaken for someone else.

Hurriedly Nessa turned and went back to the underground room. Aoife was still muttering furiously, but Nessa ignored her. She put her two arms around her mother and pulled her to her feet. Using all of her strength she hauled her mother up the steps, one by one, from the underground room. Perhaps the Viking boy was hiding out there in the shadows and he would hear them. But no, why should he come back? Surely it was better for him to limp away from a place that knew his secret. When dawn came he might be able to get a ride on a cart from some kindly person. There were many people of his colouring – Vikings by descent – who were now as Irish as the Irish themselves. He would not be questioned. He might be able to make his way back to Limerick, she thought. She didn't care. She just wanted to be rid of him. It made her sick to think of all the care that she had given him, all the tears that she had shed when she thought he was her brother. Who was he, she wondered again? How did Niall of Corcomroe and Fintan mistake him for Lochlann?

'Only a few more steps now, mother, and you'll be warm in front of the fire again, and I'll put some more salve on that eye of yours,' she whispered. Even by the pale, cold light of the moon she could see that the septic sores around her mother's burned eye were even worse.

'Come on, mother,' she said desperately. For some reason her mother was trying to pull away from her and go down into the underground room again. Nessa clung on to her frantically and managed to turn her back again towards the house. Then she had to let go of her for a moment. A flagstone placed over the hole usually disguised the way down to the underground room. Her father was very particular about this. 'You never know when we might need this place in a time of danger,' he often said. 'I only open it in front of those whom I trust.' However, while he was away, Nessa had not bothered with closing it. She had found it easier to leave the steps uncovered so that she could go down there for stores of oatmeal and butter. Now, however, she was afraid that her mother, in the blind, insane terror that seemed to possess her, might just fall down the steps and break her neck.

Quickly, using all of her strength, she dragged the flagstone back over the entrance. It fell with a thud on that silent moonlit night and for a moment her heart jumped. Perhaps the Viking boy was hiding out there in the shadows? Perhaps the noise would draw him back? Then she shook herself fiercely. That's nonsense, she thought. Why should he come back? By daylight, he would be far from Drumshee, and from the one person who knew that he was a Viking. Perhaps some charitable person would give him a lift in a cart. Perhaps he might be able to get to Limerick. He might even have some relatives or friends there. There were Viking traders in Limerick, still. Brian Boru allowed them to stay because they had many skills. She put her two arms around her mother again and held her firmly for a minute, gradually turning her towards the house. Then she dragged her over the flagstone path, around the corner of the forge, and towards the open door of the little house.

'Did I leave it as widely open as that?' said Nessa. It was strange, but she thought that she had almost closed it over, just leaving the latch undone. 'Why did I leave it open so wide? All the heat will have gone out of the room.' She said the sentences aloud for the comfort of hearing her own voice, but she knew that her mother had gone past hearing or understanding. Slowly and painfully, inch-by-inch, Nessa dragged her across the last few paces and then, once they were both through the door, she released her mother and with her two hands, slammed the door shut.

There was a soft sound from behind her – the sound of a breath suddenly sucked in. She turned around.

Chapter 9

The boy was still there! He had been crouching behind the door. But now he rose to his full height. He limped to the door and stood with his back to the latch.

And in his hand he held the sharp knife that Nessa had left beside the bread basket.

Nessa stared at him. In the silence, she could hear a strange noise: a knocking sound, a sound of bone grating against bone. It took her a moment to realise that what she could hear was the sound of the two rows of her own teeth chattering convulsively against each other. Her whole body shook and trembled. She stood and she stared. Her mother huddled in a moaning, muttering heap on the ground.

'Lochlann,' moaned Aoife in her delirium. And then, a moment later, she muttered, 'Oscar,' and then 'Nessa.'

The sound of her own name steadied Nessa. Oscar was dead and buried, Lochlann was not there either – only she was there, and only she could help her mother now.

'Fintan,' she whispered under her breath, and she uttered his name like a prayer, and like a prayer it steadied her. Ignoring the boy with the knife, she bent down and with all of her young strength managed to move her mother onto the bed beside the fire. The drink that Bridget had given her, made from willow leaves and sweetened with honey, was heating in an iron mug on a stone beside the fire and Nessa carefully propped up her mother's head and poured some down her throat. Some of it spilled, but Nessa saw Aoife's throat cords move and knew that her mother had swallowed most of it. This would help to bring the fever down and make her sleep. Carefully she lowered her mother's head back down on to the pillow of sheep's wool and pulled the bedcoverings over her. Only then did she turn to face the boy with the knife.

He was watching her closely. His blue eyes were full of life and of intelligence. He was perfectly well; she understood that now. He had just been waiting for the wound on his leg to heal and then, perhaps, one night, he would have stolen out of the house and they would have seen him no more. If only I had not spoken to him in Norse, thought Nessa. If only I had gone on treating him as if he were Lochlann. Now he will probably kill me and then my mother will die and our whole family will be gone. At that thought her blue eyes filled with tears. Hastily she blinked them away. Everything depended on her, and she had to think quickly and cleverly.

'Lochlann?' she said keeping her voice as steady as possible.

He shook his head. There was a look of amusement in his blue eyes. For a moment Nessa remembered Lochlann in a teasing mood. This boy did look like him. Perhaps it was all a bad dream, she tried to tell herself. But the knife in his hand did not move. It still pointed directly at her and she understood its menace.

'Not Lochlann.' He spoke in Norse and he spoke with assurance. He knew that he had the upper hand now. He must be pretty sure that the men had all gone.

'Who are you?' she replied in the same tongue.

He hesitated a minute and then said: 'Harald.'

'Where do you come from?'

Again he hesitated and then replied, 'The Isle of Man.'

'With Brodar?' questioned Nessa, remembering what Fintan had told her.

The boy gave a short laugh. 'With Brodar,' he confirmed. Again there was that look of intense amusement in his eyes. Slowly Nessa began to grope towards the truth.

'Brodar was killed at Clontarf,' she said hesitantly, the unfamiliar Norse words coming slowly to her tongue.

The expression on the boy's face blackened. The look of amusement vanished. The knife twitched in his hand. Suddenly he looked older – older and angrier, though perhaps there was a look of sorrow behind the anger. Nessa felt a new pang of fear but she persisted.

'Brodar killed Brian Boru, High King of Ireland,' she continued.

The boy did not reply but a flash of pride seemed to cross his face.

'And Brodar's son was killed at Clontarf, also?'

This time she was not mistaken; the boy was struggling not to laugh. He spoke with a distinct chuckle in his voice.

'Yes,' he said, 'killed at Clontarf. It is very sad.'

Nessa watched him steadily for a moment, turning the Norse words carefully over in her mind. Then, when she was ready, she spoke quickly.

'No, not killed! Brodar's son was not killed at Clontarf. You are Brodar's son!'

For a moment the fear leaped into the boy's eyes,

but then he glanced down at the knife in his hand and gave a slight laugh.

'Yes,' he said with a contemptuous shrug. 'I am Brodar's son, Harald. You are the only person to know that I am still alive so now I must kill you.'

'So you . . .' she hesitated and then started again, trying to keep her voice steady 'so you killed my brother, Lochlann?'

The boy shook his head. 'No,' he said calmly. 'I did not kill him?'

'But he is dead?'

'Yes, he is dead.' He looked at her appraisingly. 'He looked like you.'

She ignored this. 'Who killed him?' she asked.

For a moment she thought he would refuse to answer and she stared at him fiercely. It had suddenly become essential that she know the truth of her brother's death.

He shifted uneasily, transferring the whole of his weight to his uninjured leg.

'Why don't you sit down?' she asked, sinking down on to the floor beside her mother's bed. 'Bring the stool over to the door. I won't move; I promise you that.'

Keeping his eyes fixed on her and the knife pointing at her, he dragged over a stool and perched awkwardly on it. Some of the tension seemed to have gone out of him.

'Looked like you; looked like me,' he said after a pause.

'So you killed him,' she repeated.

'No,' he said briefly.

'Tell me what happened,' she said softly.

He looked at the knife in his hand and turned it over and over as if he could not quite remember why he had it. Then he looked back at her with a look of fear in his eyes.

'Keep still!' he suddenly shouted.

'Yes,' said Nessa peacefully. She had not moved, but obviously the boy's nerves were shattered. She cast a quick anxious glance at her mother. If Aoife woke now and started shouting, or even lunging at the boy, then the situation could get out of control. However, the sick woman still slept peacefully and Nessa turned her attention back to the boy.

You had Lochlann's clothes,' she said flatly.

'We had lost the battle, you know,' he said suddenly, 'nearly all of my father's Vikings were killed. The Irish were pushing us back. Our men were running into the sea, the Irish were following them and slaughtering them. The archers – the Irish archers – were sending swarms of arrows into the backs of our Viking troops.' He stopped and dipped a mug into the wooden water bucket by the door and drank thirstily. He put down the mug and swung around towards her, the knife glinting in the firelight, but Nessa did not flinch, did not move.

'I won't do anything to hurt you,' she said softly and reassuringly. 'Don't be afraid.'

He glared at her and she bit back a smile. Obviously she had hurt his pride with the word 'afraid'. However, she kept her eyes fixed on the fire and after a moment he continued with his story.

'My father, Brodar,' he continued, and now there was a note of pride in his voice. 'He was not afraid. He looked all around and he saw that no one was defending the hillside slopes. He told me to follow him. We ran up the hillside and no one followed us. "Come," said my father. "We will make our way through this wood and then we will make our way down to the city of Dublin when night falls" and that's what we did,' he added.

'And what happened then?' asked Nessa.

The boy shot her a quick glance. 'There was a tent in the middle of the wood,' he said rapidly. 'There was an old, old man standing outside it with a gold crown on his head and beside him was a boy of my own age.'

'It was my brother,' whispered Nessa.

'Your brother was very brave. He threw himself in front of the old king. My father shouted: "It's Brian Boru, himself!"'

'And what happened then?'

The boy shrugged. 'My father lifted his battle-axe; he aimed at the old king. He wanted to kill him – just him. You know there was still a chance that the battle might have turned. If only Sitric of Dublin had come to our aid, instead of staying behind the walls of Dublin. If the old king, Brian Boru were to be killed, his followers would have lost their heart.'

'So he killed him?'

'Not straight away.'

'Tell me,' she said again. 'Tell me the truth.'

'Your brother jumped in front of the king. He swung his sword. He wounded me on the leg. My father had to kill him, or he would have killed me. Your brother died immediately; he did not suffer,' the boy gave a quick glance at Nessa's face. He looked awkward and embarrassed.

Nessa bowed her head. It did not comfort her that Lochlann died a hero. That was men's thoughts, but it did comfort her to know that he had not died in agony.

'It was no good, though,' she said dully. 'Brian

Boru was killed anyway. Lochlann should have run away.'

'No,' said Harald strongly. 'If he had run away, he could never have lived with himself afterwards. He was a man that day and he did his best for his king. He will go to Valhalla – or wherever you Christians go when you die.'

'And the king?' asked Nessa. 'What happened to Brian Boru?'

'My father hit him on the head with the battle axe, but Brian Boru had time to get ready while Lochlann, your brother, had been protecting him. He swung his sword. My father's blow hit him on the head and at the same moment Brian Boru's sword sliced off both of my father's legs.'

'Oh,' said Nessa. She caught her breath. The pain on the boy's face was almost impossible to watch.

'He was dying,' said Harald dully. 'But before he died, he found strength to think of me. "They will come soon, these Irish," he said to me. "I hear their voices." And then he shouted at me: "Quick, change clothes with that Irish boy. You can't run away with that wound on your leg. This will give you a chance. He looks like your twin. Who knows," my father said, "he may even be a relation of yours – my father's twin brother was a boat-builder on the Shannon near Limerick."'

'Yes,' said Nessa, 'he may have been a relation.' She tried to remember the old stories that her grandfather had told her, but nothing seemed to come to her mind except the image of Lochlann dying there on the hillside above Clontarf. 'And what happened then?' she asked dully.

'My father,' said the boy with a catch in his voice, 'my father was filled with a terrible energy, though I could see the mark of death in his face. "Strip off his tunic and his cloak and his pouch," he shouted. "Take off your helmet and your armour. Put them on him. Quick. I hear their voices!" So I stripped the body . . .your brother, I mean − and I dressed him in my armour and I pulled on his tunic and his cloak and I buckled his pouch around my waist and then the Irish came bursting in.'

'And they thought you were Lochlann,' said Nessa.

'I fainted, I think,' said the boy hesitantly. 'I don't remember much else. I think leeches − healers − came and looked at me. I remember that. I didn't know what to do. I just lay there with my eyes shut. Then I was lifted on to a stretcher and there were long days travelling on the road. I didn't know what to do' he repeated. 'I knew what they would do to me if they discovered that I was Brodar's son. I heard them talking.' He swallowed and then said: 'They talked of pulling out the intestines of the still-living man and winding them around a tree.'

Nessa clenched her hands tightly. There was a note of hysterical fear in the boy's voice. 'Never trust an animal when it's frightened,' her father had often told her. 'Even the quietest cow or horse can kill if it is frightened enough.'

Nessa stared at the boy and at the sharp knife that trembled in his hand. Would he kill? Of course he would, she answered the question in her mind. He would have killed many people. He would have been one of the warriors for the last few years.

'I'll help you to get away,' she said softly and soothingly.

He glared at her. 'How?' he asked abruptly, and then with a sudden gleam of hope, 'Have you got a horse?'

'Yes,' she said, and then, 'no.' She shook her head. 'It's not here just now,' she said, 'but soon I will have it back,' she added.

'Where is this horse?' he asked aggressively.

Where was her father's grey stallion, she wondered, feeling bewildered for a moment. Then she remembered. Fintan had taken him to her father's graveside, as was the tradition. The stallion would have stood there over the grave as his master was buried.

'I will take him back with me and my father will look after him until you decide what to do with him,' Fintan had said. It had been understood that Nessa would not ride the stallion. Her father had forbidden her to do so and not even to Fintan had she confided that she often rode the horse whenever her father was not around and her mother was locked in the black claws of depression.

'I suppose the stallion will have to be sold,' she had said to Fintan.

'Your father said the stallion was a very difficult, dangerous horse and needed all of his bulk of muscle to manage him,' Fintan had agreed. 'Neither you, nor your mother, would be able to ride him,' he had added, though he had often seen how the horse was docile and easy to handle when Nessa fed or brushed him.

She had nodded in agreement. He would fetch a sum of money that might keep her and her mother in food. She loved him; he was a beautiful horse, but she would have to sell him

'The horse is over at the farm by Lough Fergus,' she said aloud. 'Fintan will bring back my father's horse, when he comes back with the healer for my mother. Will you be able to ride him? He is very difficult to ride.'

'I can ride any horse in the world,' he boasted.

She shrugged. 'Well then you can have him when Fintan comes back,' she said.

Harald shook his head firmly. 'No,' he said flatly, 'you will betray me when your friend comes back. You will not be able to keep the secret. I plan to kill you before they arrive.' He stared at her aggressively and she stared back.

He doesn't mean it, she thought. He is frightened and he is ashamed of being frightened and that makes him aggressive. She smiled at him.

'That would not help you,' she said firmly. 'You're very lame. You won't be able to get away from here without a horse. We'll have to think of something else.'

He thought for a moment. 'How far away is this farm?' he asked.

'Only about half a mile?' she answered.

'Get the horse now,' he said. 'If you can bring me a horse tonight I'll ride away and you'll never see me again. You can pretend that your brother went away, that he was cured.'

Would he really ride away? she wondered. Would he really trust her to lie for him? She looked at him doubtfully. 'But what about my mother?' she asked.

'How can I go to the farm when she is so ill? I can't take her with me.'

'Leave her here,' he said briskly. A smile tugged at the corners of his mouth.

Nessa knew that expression. Lochlann used to wear an expression like that when he knew he was going to get his own way. She looked at her mother worriedly. Aoife seemed sunk in a deep sleep. Was it possible to do as the boy asked, she wondered? The stallion would walk with her; he would give no trouble. She would not attempt to ride him through the darkness, but the walk would not take long. It would probably take less than an hour – possibly only half an hour to bring the stallion back. Her greatest worry was her mother.

Harald followed the direction of her eyes. The mocking angry look disappeared from his face. 'I'm sorry about your mother,' he said gently. 'She is very ill, I know that, but you can trust me to look after her. If she wakes and cries, I'll give her some of that fever drink. I won't speak to her. She will think it is you. She is blind, is she not? She won't know that you are gone and, in any case, if you leave now you will probably be back before she wakens.'

'I'll go,' said Nessa suddenly making up her mind. 'I won't be long. While I'm gone you can be preparing yourself for the journey. You can put some fresh salve on your wound and here are some clean strips of linen to tie it up with . . . ' she hesitated, but then resolutely went on, '. . . and you can take Lochlann's clothes and his boots from that chest over there. He will not need them now and they may keep you safe as well as warm on your journey.

'Thank you,' he said his white teeth flashing in a smile. 'Thank you very much.' And then, in a low voice, he added 'I'm sorry I threatened you with the knife. I feared that what happened to my father might happen to me. I fear it all the time. I dream about it sometimes.' He looked away in an embarrassed fashion as if he feared that he had said too much.

'I'll go now,' said Nessa taking her cloak from the back of the door. 'You can keep the knife,' she added. 'Stick it your belt when you are dressed. We have many knives here.' Slowly and deliberately she went over to the square storage hole by the chimney, took a wickedly sharp knife from there, tucked it into her pouch, smiled sweetly at Harald, went through the door and out into the night. Of course she already had a knife in her pouch, but she enjoyed the memory of his astonished face. Obviously, he thought that because she was a girl she would be afraid of him.

Chapter 10

When Nessa stepped outside the gates of the fort, for a moment she hesitated. If she turned left and crossed the Togher field she could get to Fintan's place more quickly. On the other hand, the Togher Road skirted the bog and if the moon went behind the clouds she might risk going astray. No, she decided, it would be safer to go straight ahead down to the Fergus and to walk along the broad riverside path.

The Fergus was in full flood after the heavy rains of springtime, and the merry noise of the river crashing down over the little waterfall lifted Nessa's spirits. Perhaps the night, which had started so badly, might end well after all. She would bring back the stallion, Harald would ride away, and the healer would find what was wrong with her mother and then, her thoughts ran on, she would get married to Fintan, and the forge at Drumshee would live again.

For a moment she felt guilty that she could plan like this when her father and her brother had been killed at Clontarf, but she pushed the thought aside

98

– nothing she could do would help them now – and she began to run the last few hundred yards between the river and Fintan's farm.

The little house was in darkness; that was good. The household must be in bed and asleep. Nessa had no desire to have to invent an explanation for removing the stallion in the middle of the night. She crept up to the stable and, by the clear light of the moon, lifted the latch and went inside.

Fintan's friendly old horse was not there – Fintan must still be at Kincora – but the stallion was in the stall and he swung his head around and glared at her. The fierce look in his eye made Nessa hesitate. Why didn't I bring some oats in my pouch, she thought. She looked quickly around the stable; the best she could find was some hay, so she pulled out a sweet-smelling handful and stretched her hand straight out, palm uppermost. She held it as steadily as she could until the stallion bent his great head and delicately lipped the hay from her hand. There was a curry brush lying in a nook in the wall so Nessa took it and started to brush the dusty coat, starting at the hindquarters and gradually moving forward until she reached the muscular neck. Transferring the brush to her left hand without ceasing the steady even rhythm of her strokes, she gently took hold of the bridle. The horse stepped forward. She put the brush away, walked another few steps, and the horse followed again. They were through the door now and out into the moonlight. An owl hooted overhead, startling the stallion, but Nessa spoke softly to him. He turned and sniffed her shoulder and seemed to recognise his master's blood because he walked steadily by her side as she went through the gate and crossed over to the path beside the River Fergus.

Nessa's return journey took longer than the journey out to Lough Fergus. She dared not rush the horse and panic him. Slowly and steadily she walked along the path, stroking him from time to time and always talking to him in a slow soothing stream of words. Her own mind, she felt to her surprise, was also soothed and calmed during this moonlit walk. It was only now that she fully realised the intensity of her tension during the last week. First there had been the wait for news of the battle, then had come the death of her father, then the frightening realisation that her mother was now, no longer, completely sane and then last of all, the discovery that Lochlann was not Lochlann, but a Viking boy who threatened to kill her.

When they reached the ford, Nessa turned and walked up the hill towards the fort. The wind was in the east so the humming noise of the river filled her ears as she climbed the steep meadows. She could see a light from the little house looking a friendly orange in the pale white light of the moon. The boy, Harald, would be ready now; he had had plenty of time. I'll give him some bread to take with him, she thought. He'll meet plenty of streams where he can drink, but it would be best not to ask anyone for food – best if he spoke to no one until he reached Limerick. For a moment she almost felt sorry that he was going. I'll miss talking to him, she thought, but then she shook herself with horror. Why on earth should she feel like that? This boy was an enemy and he had threatened to kill her. His father had killed Lochlann, and also King Brian Boru.

Nessa had left the heavy iron gates to the fort open, so she and the horse were able to walk straight through. It was just as they came through, that the hum from the river left her ears and was replaced by something else. A terrible noise was coming from the house. Her mother was screaming.

Hardly knowing what she was doing, Nessa tied the stallion to the ring in front of the forge. Then she pulled out the sharp knife from her pouch, lifted the door latch quietly and then burst into the room.

For a moment she thought the boy was killing her mother and her knife was raised and ready to plunge into his back as she came up behind him. She had never killed anything – not even a hare, but for a moment she was ready to kill. Then she realised that Harald had his arms around her mother; that he was holding her, and murmuring to her. He was singing, no – not singing, just a wordless low crooning. He looked up at her with relief in his face. His eyes did not go to the knife so she slid it back into her pouch and bent over her mother.

'Mother,' she said. 'It's me. It's Nessa? What's the matter?'

Aoife was well beyond any reply or any recognition of her daughter. She was trying to bang her head against the stone wall of the cottage. Nessa could see the livid bruise on her forehead. Harald was holding her with all of his strength, but Aoife pulled and twisted in his grasp. Her breath came in great pants and her face, except for the flaming red of the sore around the eye, was grey and sunken.

'Have you tried the fever drink?' whispered Nessa in Harald's ear. He shook his head.

'I couldn't let go of her,' he muttered. 'She just suddenly woke up and started screaming and then she started to bang her head against the wall. I thought she would knock her brains out.'

Nessa watched her mother as Harald spoke.

Although he spoke in such a low tone he was just beside her. However, Aoife showed no reaction whatsoever to the strange voice or to the strange language. She had gone beyond recognition of strangers; she had even gone beyond recognition of her own daughter. Nothing now existed for her but pain.

Nessa went over to the fire and dipped the mug into the mixture of willow leaves and honey. She held it to Aoife's lips, but the woman was unable to swallow. Her teeth were clenched together in agony and the liquid just spilled down her chin when Nessa tried to pour some into her mouth.

'Get me a small piece of wood,' said Harald. 'I'll try to force her mouth open.' He spoke in normal tones now. It was obvious that Aoife was locked away in her own world of pain and fever and that she knew no one. Nessa went over to the dresser and took the spoon made from alder wood that her mother used to stir the cream. She brought it back over to the bed and handed it to Harald. All her movements felt stiff and jerky and her legs could hardly support her. She sat down on the end of the bed and just looked at him. His face was white and he looked frightened also. He tried to smile at her, but his lips trembled. He took his right arm away from around Aoife and gently squeezed her cheeks trying vainly to make her open her mouth. Aoife screamed and twisted her head away. She threw herself forward on the bed, and twisted again so that her legs were on the floor. Then she started to bang the back of her head on the heather-filled mattress.

'Let me hold her,' said Nessa urgently. She placed the mug on the ground beside the bed and put her two arms around her mother trying to pull her up.

Harald took his other arm away and stood up, the alder spoon in one hand. 'Take care,' he began to say, 'she's very . . .'

Before the last word was uttered Aoife suddenly tore herself away and hurtled herself across the room. The door was still standing open and she was through it before Nessa realised what was happening. It took her a moment to get to her feet, but in that time Harald was already through the door shouting in Norse: 'Come back, come back!'

'Mother, mother,' screamed Nessa stumbling over the mug on the floor. Her foot slipped on its rounded sides and she fell heavily, her cheekbone crashing against the stone-flagged floor. She was up in a moment, feeling the warm blood flowing down her face. 'Mother, mother,' she screamed as she rushed through the door. If Aoife had any understanding left, she would be terrified at this voice shouting to her in Norse.

But all was dark outside the little house. The storm clouds had gathered over the moon, there was a strong wind blowing from the west and heavy drops of rain fell on Nessa's face. 'Mother,' she said again, but she could hear no sound.

'She's gone,' said Harald's voice from beside her. 'I think she went through the gate. I can't see. We'll have to get a light. Wait here.' And then he limped back into the little house.

Nessa did not listen. She ran to the gate still calling. She was crying now and tears, blood and rain ran down her face and dripped off her chin. It was like a terrible dream. Where could her mother have gone? She listened intently, but it was impossible to hear anything except the noise of the wind buffeting the old ash tree outside the walls and the sound of the rain beating on the stone-flagged fort.

'I've got a torch,' said Harald from beside her.

Nessa glanced at him. He had kindled a resin-filled stump of pine tree in the fire and it blazed with a soft orange glow. He held it up, but the light stretched a pitiably short distance of only a few paces. All around the hillside was black and filled with the wind and the rain. The stallion tied to the ring outside the forge neighed suddenly and angrily.

'Where could she have gone?' asked Harald urgently.

'Are you sure she went through the gate?' asked Nessa. He turned the light towards her.

'You're bleeding,' he exclaimed. He fumbled with his left hand in his pouch and brought out a square of soft linen – Lochlann's, thought Nessa, but when he mopped her bleeding cheekbone he did it more gently than Lochlann would have done. The stallion neighed again.

'Perhaps she is in the forge,' said Nessa.

'Perhaps,' said Harald. There was a note of relief in his voice.

Nessa rushed forward ignoring the stallion and Harald followed her, holding the torch so that her path was lit up.

The door was stiff and swollen – it had not been opened since Oscar had left for that ill-fated march to the battle at Clontarf – but Harald put his shoulder to it, pointed the torch in and swung its light around the walls. There was no one there; Nessa hardly needed to look. The stiff door had told its own story.

'Is there any other place that she might go to?' asked Harald urgently. 'Somewhere that she might feel . . .' he hesitated and then finished in a low voice, 'somewhere she might feel safe.'

My mother is mad, thought Nessa dully. How can I see into the mind of a mad person? Then a hot wave of shame came over her. How could she think like that? Her mother was ill. She was to blame that Aoife was so ill. She should have looked after the sore around the eye better. She should not have allowed it to develop into an abscess. Perhaps if she had prayed more all of this would never have happened.

'There's the statue of St Brigid,' she said suddenly, aloud. 'It's under the ash tree outside the fort. She might have gone there. She likes to pray there.'

'Show me,' said Harald. He put his left arm across her shoulders and held her to him for a second and released her. Suddenly she felt warmed and comforted. She slipped her hand into his and led him through the gate and then turned to the left, following the bulk of the wall until they came to the ash tree.

'The statue is under the tree,' she said pointing. But her mother would not be there. She knew that. Harald held the spluttering torch low down and shone it under the bare black-tipped branches of the ash tree. The little statue was there, made from stone – the image of an old woman covered in a cloak, her face half-hidden in the hood, her eyes, sunken and wise – she had been there for a thousand years and those who lived in the fort had always worshipped and prayed to her. Nessa felt like throwing herself on her knees and praying for help, but they dared not waste time. She turned away and Harald came with her.

At that moment, a great gust of wind swept up the hill and the flame from the torch wavered and went out. Nessa stood. What could they do now? Her throat was hoarse with calling for her mother, but once again she raised the cry. It was useless; she knew that. The wind was blowing very strongly now and her words were swept out of her mouth and blown across the hilltop.

But then the wind blew the heavy black cloud aside from the moon and suddenly it shone out strongly making the raindrops on the grass sparkle in its light. It lit up the tree and the walls and cast deep black shadows below them. It lit up the fields and the hedges and it lit up the cattle drinking-pond.

'Look,' said Harald.

And Nessa looked and she began to run.

The centre of the drinking-pond was stained and clotted with clumps of marsh irises and waterweed, but the edge was normally clear.

But tonight, something lay there. A black shape of wet clothing.

Chapter 11

Afterwards, Nessa could never clearly remember what happened next. She remembered being back in the little house. She remembered holding her mother's soaking wet body in her arms. She remembered the sound of her own heartbroken sobs, she remembered the feeling of a terrible guilt – but she never remembered the lifting of her mother's drowned body from the pond.

Harald had done it, of course. Harald that night took the place of her father. He was the one who held her, who comforted her. Harald piled the fire high with sticks and pieces of turf, wrapped a warm sheepskin around her, bathed her cheek and put ointment on the wound and brought her back to sanity in the end. As the pale light of dawn began to stain the sky over the hill to the east he eventually found a means to soothe over the raw edges of her terrible grief.

'Nessa, your mother could not have lived much longer,' he said. 'And during the few last days that she lived, she would have been in that terrible pain.'

'How do you know,' sobbed Nessa.

'I have seen men like that,' he said, 'men who had received a head wound and one – my friend – my best friend – he was the same age as me – he got an arrow in his eye during a battle at Inverness.' He stared into the fire and Nessa turned her eyes from the dead body of her mother and looked at him.

'What happened to him?' she asked.

He shrugged. 'He went blind. And then the terrible pain began.'

'What happened?' she asked again.

'My father killed him with his knife,' he said shortly. 'He thrust his knife into my friend's heart. My father was a merciful man,' he added as he got up and went to the window. 'It was the right thing to do,' he said over his shoulder, throwing open the shutters and leaning his chest and arms out into the morning breeze.

Nessa could think of nothing to say. A protest rose within her and then she shut her mouth firmly. Harald loved his father very much; she knew that. She did not want to hurt Harald. She remembered all his kindness to her during the long night and she did not wish to speak the sentence that rose to her lips: 'Your father was a Viking barbarian.'

But was he, she wondered, looking at the quiet

face of her mother. Was it right or wrong to kill someone who was in agony, someone who would die soon in any case? The Christian law said it was wrong – but was it? Would it have been right to keep her mother alive for days, weeks, perhaps? Could anything, anyone, have saved her? If the healer from Kincora had arrived in time, could he have saved her mother? Or would it just have been days and weeks of useless treatments and an agonising death at the end? She thought she knew the answer to that. For the first time she began to feel a little better. She turned towards Harald.

'Harald,' she said softly.

'Hush,' he said. 'Listen!'

She walked across and stood beside him. The wind had died down and it was a calm sunny morning. In the still morning air sounds carried well and she knew this sound: 'It's the cuckoo,' she said.

'Not that,' he said impatiently. 'Listen!' he repeated. And then she heard it – under the two-note call of the cuckoo, she heard it – the sound that she had been listening for all day yesterday. It was the sound of men on horseback splashing through the ford at the bottom of the hill.

Dumb with dismay, Nessa turned to stare at Harald. She had longed for this moment, but now all that she could think of was that Fintan's return would bring deadly danger to this Viking boy who had shared her sorrows and who helped her and done all that he could for her mother.

'Quick,' she said. 'You must go. Go now. Take the stallion and go,' she repeated urgently dragging him through the door and outside towards the forge. 'Go north until you are well clear of Drumshee, then turn east until you come to Quinn's Lake and then turn and keep heading south. Follow the River Fergus until you come to Limerick.' Suddenly Nessa stopped half-way across the yard. 'Wait, let me untie the stallion – go back inside and put some bread in your pouch. I'll hold the stallion while you mount.'

He obeyed her, bending his fair young head to go back into the house. Nessa went over and stroked the stallion, murmuring to him and untying the bridle from the ring.

And then, from down the meadow, less than a hundred paces away, came a shout.

'Nessa,' called Fintan. 'Nessa, is that you? Are you all right, dear heart? We got caught in a storm and had to shelter for the night.'

And then Harald came back out again, clutching the sharp knife.

'It's too late,' he said, his breath coming in quick

short gasps. 'It's no good. They'll see me. They'll see the stallion. They'll kill the horse from under me with their throwing spears.'

'Wait,' she said. Suddenly her mind was working properly. 'Wait!'

She dropped the stallion's bridle and gave him a sharp slap on the rump. He galloped forward and burst through the gate, running downhill. It was just what Nessa hoped he would do. It would gain her a few vital moments. She could already hear the surprised shouts of Fintan and the other men.

'Quick!' she said as Harald came towards her. She rushed around the corner of the forge pulling him by the hand. Rapidly she tore up the stone slab, bruising and tearing her fingernails, and pushed him towards the steps. 'Go down,' she hissed. 'There's a room down there. Stay there until I come for you. No one will find you there. No one knows of this place. This place is the secret of Drumshee.'

He went down. He went as quickly as he could with his lame leg. But he stopped for one thing. Nessa felt his lips press down on hers and then he was limping rapidly down the steps. As soon as his head was level with the ground she dragged the slab back into place and pushed the grasses over its mossy surface. And then she went and stood by the gate feeling suddenly drained of all feeling.

They were still trying to capture the stallion down in the meadow. Fintan was there, Niall of Corcomroe was there also, a young lad with him, and an older man in flowing robes. That must be the healer, she thought sadly. Well, he has had a wasted journey. Her mother was dead and she dared not let him see Harald. The healer was taking no part in the chase, she noticed. He looked old, with a strangely yellow skin. He sat on his horse and watched the others. She should go and help, she thought, but her legs refused to carry her. Without the support of the gate she would have sunken to the ground.

'We'll try to drive him through the gate, Nessa,' shouted Fintan. 'Stand back, sweetheart. Stand on the inside. Slam the gate once we are through. Don't try to touch him, yourself. I'll handle him.'

Dear Fintan, she thought wearily. He was always thinking about her. Always ready to protect her. She had no fear of the stallion at this moment. She almost felt that it would be easier to lie down and let the stallion trample her to death. She could feel herself sliding down. Her face was cold and there was a strange mist in front of her eyes. But then she shook herself. Harald, she said to herself. She had to get Harald away safely. She had seen the terrible look of fear in his eyes when he spoke of his father's dreadful death. She could not allow him to be caught and killed – perhaps to be tortured first – the men would want vengeance for the death of Brian Boru. There was only one way for him to escape with his lame leg. The stallion was his only means of escape. She would have to help the men to get the stallion back.

She looked down the hill. The plan was a good one, but they were exciting the horse too much. Again and again the stallion foiled their attempts to make a circle around him and drive him back up the hill. She took another quick look. Yes, she would have time. She rushed back into the house. The solemn figure of her dead mother was lying there in the corner of the room and a sudden memory came to her of how Harald had cradled Aoife in his arms, had helped the mother, and then, after the terrible death, how he had helped and comforted the daughter. She had to do her best to save him.

Swiftly she went over to the wooden box by the door, flipped its lid open, ladled out a measure of oats and went back to the gate. Steadily she walked through the gate until she was well outside. The stallion must not feel trapped, she thought.

'Here boy, here,' she called keeping her voice steady. The stallion paused in his mad circling and glanced back at her. He neighed, but it was more a neigh of greeting than of anger, and once again she called: 'Here boy, here,' and this time she threw a handful of oats on the ground. He paused again and then seemed to hesitate. After what seemed to be a long time, slowly and hesitantly, he moved up the hill

'Keep back, Fintan,' she called. 'Keep everyone back. Leave him to me. He knows me.'

She did not look to see whether her command was heeded. Still calling she moved backwards, scattering oats in a thick line back through the gate and right up to the door of the forge. And then she waited.

And yes, she had guessed correctly. The stallion was hungry. Normally he was left loose overnight in the little field, the Cathaireen, beside the fort. Normally he would have eaten his fill of grass when dawn came. But last night he had been left tied up so he had not been able to feed and now he was very hungry. He moved along the line of oats sucking them up into his mouth. He did not even hesitate when he came through the gate but continued along the flagstone path. Nessa did not move. She prayed that no one would shout or move towards the gate. She knew this horse. He could only be coaxed, not driven.

'Good boy, good boy,' she kept on saying in a low steady voice until he came near to her. Then she reached out. He flinched and moved aside. He did not want to be caught. Once again she stretched out her hand, but this time towards his rump and she stroked him gently still continuing to murmur to him. He stood very still and turned his noble head towards her. She moved her hand up and stroked his neck, then carefully took the bridle in her left hand and knotted it to the ring. She continued to stroke and murmur for a few minutes and then left him and walked to the gate.

'You can all come in now,' she said, and was surprised to find how steady her voice sounded.

'Nessa, how did the stallion get loose? I left him in the stable at Lough Fergus. I can't understand how he got loose!'

Fintan did not kiss her; Nessa was glad of that. She still tasted Harald's kiss on her lips.

'I don't know,' she said. To her relief her voice sounded innocently puzzled. 'He just ran in the gate. I was just trying to catch him when you arrived,' she added, surprised and pleased that the lie came so quickly and fluently.

Fintan nodded. He was easy to deceive. He did not puzzle or worry about things as she did. It was

Niall of Corcomroe who spoke next.

'This is the healer,' he said. 'He has spent many years across the sea. He has great skill. May we come into your house?'

Nessa nodded and stood aside. They dismounted from their horses, each man handing the bridles to the young lad and then bent their heads and went inside. She followed them. The fire had burned away during the long night of agony; the little house was dark and when she went in she could see them blinking. There was little room there with the three men filling the space and she hesitated at the doorway wondering what to say.

Niall turned around towards her and stood back, flattening himself against the wall. Fintan was looking towards the fireplace with a puzzled air. The healer stood with his chin sunk on his chest looking weary and uninterested. There was a silence. Fintan was staring around the room; he knew it well, of course. The hangings, which screened off the sleeping places, were all open. She could see his eyes go to her parents' bed near the fireplace, to her own bed and then to Lochlann's place. He moved forward and then stopped with a startled sound.

There was no doubt that Aoife was dead. Nessa had stripped the soaking wet clothes from her and had covered the body in a linen winding sheet. All the angry redness had gone from the sore around her eye and now it was a dull bruised purple. The face itself was a waxen white.

It was the healer who spoke eventually. 'The woman is dead,' he said flatly.

'Yes,' said Nessa. There was no more emotion in her voice than there had been in his.

'What happened?' he asked.

'She was in terrible pain,' said Nessa dully. 'She was trying to bang her head against the wall. I tried to stop her.'

The healer moved forward then. He dropped to his knees beside the body. For a moment Nessa thought he was going to pray, but he reached out with long finger and thumb and opened the eye.

'Ah,' he said rising to his feet again and wiping his hand on his long robe. 'The abscess went to the brain.'

'That would kill her?' asked Niall.

The healer shrugged. 'You cannot live if the brain dies.'

I'll leave it at that, thought Nessa. She had been going to tell them of how her mother in her agony had rushed out of the house and thrown herself into the pond, but she decided to say no more. She wanted no difficult questions about how she managed to carry her mother back to the house. She never wanted to speak about that terrible night again.

'I must bury her, Fintan,' she said. 'Will you see the priest at Clogher. I would like to bury her this morning. Will you do that for me.'

He nodded. He seemed dazed. Niall of Corcomroe also seemed not to know what to say. The healer had already turned around and had gone outside the house. Through the open door Nessa could see him reach up for the bridle of his horse. No doubt, he would stay at Niall of Corcomroe's fine house for a few days and then ride back to Kincora.

'Go now, Fintan,' she said urgently hearing the hint of a sob in her voice. 'Go now. I want to be alone with my mother for the last hour.'

He turned and went out of the house. He was always obedient to her. Niall followed him. They were all mounted on their horses when suddenly Fintan turned to her with shock on his face.

'Nessa,' he said. 'What about Lochlann? What has happened to Lochlann?'

Chapter 12

Even the healer roused himself at that question. 'Yes,' he said. 'What about the wounded boy, the boy who slept, but had no fever? Where is he?' he turned to Niall for an explanation.

'The boy!' exclaimed Niall. 'Of course, I had forgotten about the boy. The girl's brother.'

'King Teige was very insistent that I should see him,' said the healer in a complaining voice. 'That was why I came. King Teige said that the boy had been injured defending his father. He was the only Irish man with King Brian when he was killed by the Viking. King Teige wanted him healed and brought back to Kincora. The bard, Mac Liag, is composing a poem about the battle of Clontarf and he wishes to talk to this boy and hear what happened in the last moments of the great Brian Boru.'

'Yes, of course,' said Niall hurriedly. He swung around to face Nessa. 'Where is Lochlann?' he asked sharply.

'Where is Lochlann, Nessa?' repeated Fintan when she said nothing.

121

Nessa stared dumbly at them. What could she say? Her mind suddenly went blank.

'Nessa,' cried Fintan. 'What happened to Lochlann? He's not dead, is he?'

Yes, he is, responded Nessa's thoughts. Yes, Lochlann is dead. He died at Clontarf. They are all dead: father, mother and brother. She longed to tell the truth, she longed for Fintan and Niall to take the burden from her, but she could not do it. The thought of the terror on Harald's face, that fair-skinned young face, so like Lochlann's and so like her own, made her resolved never to betray him.

'He went away,' she said vaguely, feeling her heart jump and flutter within her.

'Went away!' echoed Niall incredulously.

'But, Nessa,' said Fintan, 'how could he go away? How did he do it? With a wound like that on his leg, he would not have been able to walk!'

'When did he go away?' asked the healer, his eyes suddenly sharp and interested.

When, thought Nessa? Her thoughts frantically scurried around like a nest of mice between the paws of a cat.

'Last night,' she said eventually.

'Last night! After your mother's death?' It was Niall who asked the question, but Nessa kept her eyes fixed on the healer's face.

'Yes,' she said finally. It seemed the easiest thing to say.

'But what did he say?' asked Fintan. 'Where was he going?'

'He didn't say anything,' said Nessa desperately. Her imagination refused to allow her to invent any further story.

'You mean he just got up and went?' asked Niall sharply.

'Yes,' said Nessa, and then, as they all continued to stare at her, she added, 'he just got up and pulled on his *léine* and his *brat* and then he left. I was busy with my mother so I just let him go.'

'You mean he just went!' repeated Niall. He stared at her, his face puzzled.

'The boy's mind has gone,' said the healer decisively. 'That must be it. I thought it was a strange case when you told me of it. You said there was no fever and yet the boy just lay there and made no sound and gave no signal. The son's mind went as surely as the mother's did. There may be some weakness in the family that makes the brain go under stress.' And with that he moved a step nearer to Nessa and seemed to study her with great interest.

Perhaps he thinks my mind is gone also, thought Nessa.

'We'd better search for him,' said Niall decisively. 'He can't have got far. He is probably somewhere quite near. Fintan, you know the place. You search around the buildings and the walls. Colm,' he said to the young lad, 'you go down by the river and search there.'

'No,' screamed Nessa. 'No! We must bury my mother. We must do it now this morning. We must do it now. Don't delay. I can't bear it any longer. I can't have her body in the house any longer. I'll go mad if she isn't buried now.'

Quickly she covered her face with her hands and began to sob. The sounds came easily to her and, after a minute of pretence, suddenly all the terrible sorrows and troubles of the past week swept over her and she wept without restraint. She could feel the tears pouring out through her fingers and running down the backs of her hands. Her whole body was racked with sobs. After a moment, she felt herself in Fintan's arms.

'Tell them to leave me alone, Fintan,' she cried. 'Just let me bury my mother. Let me have some peace.'

She continued to sob, but under the noise of her sobs, she heard the healer say: 'Best to give her own way. Let the burial take place as soon as possible. She, also, may lose her wits if we deny her this now.'

This underground room is pretty cold and damp, thought Harald, after five minutes. He dragged himself up the steps, going slowly and making sure that he made no noise. When his head reached the flagstone he stopped and listened very carefully. Yes, he could hear voices. He understood very little of the language, but he could hear a man's voice loud and sharp and then the soft sound of Nessa's voice. Then came another voice – more questions, and then the sound of Nessa's weeping. He clenched his hands. Why were they making her cry? What was that Fintan doing? Why did he not stand up for her?

Suddenly Harald drew in a breath. I love that girl, he thought. He had often scorned other warriors – lovesick fools, his father used to call them. He smiled – he didn't care. He remembered how he had held Nessa and comforted her last night and he wished he could be with her again. Perhaps she would send that Fintan away, and the other men, too. And then he would hold her in his arms again and tell her that he loved her. He pressed his ear to the stone slab once more. There seemed to be some heavy rumbling noise and the sharp clop of horse hoofs on the cobbles, and then silence. They were gone!

Immediately Harald's fingers were at the flagstone.

He lifted it slightly. But then he heard Fintan's voice and dropped it down immediately. He could hear the voice again and then the high neigh of the stallion.

'May the hammer of Thor crush you,' Harald muttered in the darkness. 'You are going to take my horse away.' For a moment he stood fuming. He felt like going out and challenging Fintan. How was he going to escape if he did not have the stallion? He could not walk far with his wounded leg. He clenched his hands and then unclenched them again. He needed to think clearly if he was going to escape. If Fintan were still there, the other men would not have gone far. He would have to be patient. He would have to wait until Nessa came for him.

Harald moved back down the steps again. He was almost sure that all the men were gone now, but it was stupid to take the risk of being discovered. Perhaps only one or two of them had gone. He had little idea of how many men had arrived. He just had a confused notion of voices and shouts as Nessa had released the stallion and then the sound of her voice, soft and insistent in his ear. Yes, it would be best to be down in the darkness there in case anyone came. He took the knife from his pouch and held it in front of him, wishing it were a battle axe or even a sword.

I wonder why Nessa has not come, he thought

five minutes later. The men must be well out of sight. Perhaps that Fintan stayed behind. Harald was surprised how jealous the thought made him. He had seen Nessa in Fintan's arms while he lay on the bed pretending to sleep, pretending to be her brother. He set his jaw determinedly. He was used to having his own way – Harald Strong-Will, his father had called him. Surely Nessa must prefer him, a Viking warrior, to that country blacksmith!

After another quarter of an hour, Harald had grown impatient and by the time an hour had elapsed he felt as if he would die if he stayed any longer in this cold damp darkness.

'It's funny,' he muttered to himself. 'The air is good here, and yet very little air can get through that flagstone.' He dragged himself up the steps again and held up his mouth to the stone slab. He was right. The stone fitted so well that not a glimmer of light came through it and the air at the top of the steps seemed slightly staler than the air in the room itself.

'That's it, then,' he said under his breath. 'There must be another way out of this place.'

He limped down the steps again. If only I had a light, he thought impatiently, but at the same time he began to move cautiously around the room.

'Here's the wall next to the steps,' he said. This

time he spoke aloud; he was confident that no one could hear him. 'Now let's see the shape of the room.'

With his hands on the rough stones of the wall he moved around step-by-step leaning his weight on his out-stretched arms. His leg ached fiercely; it was still not used to movement, but he ignored it. It would soon get strong again.

'That's one corner,' he grunted and shuffled awkwardly to avoid a wooden barrel.

'And here's the second corner,' he said after another minute.

And then, suddenly, the wall ended. He overbalanced and lay splayed out on the rough stone floor. For a moment he stayed there gasping with the pain of his injured leg, but then he struggled to his feet again. Soft damp air blew against his face.

'That's it,' he said with triumph. 'This must lead to the outside.'

The passageway was barely wide enough for a man. Harald felt his shoulders brush against each side and after a few steps he had to lower his head.

'They must be a race of midgets, these Irish,' he said with scorn, trying to distract himself from the pain of his wounded leg. 'May Loki, the God of Mischief, curse the man who made this tunnel,' he added as his head crashed against a low stone. 'I'm going to have to crawl,' he muttered after a few more minutes. 'This tunnel is getting lower and lower.'

Crawling was agony but he hardly felt the pain now. The damp wind was blowing strongly in his face and he knew it would not be long before he was out in the open again. He was sick of being in the house, sick of pretending to be ill, sick of lying on his back. He wanted to be out. He wished that it had all been a bad dream. He shut his eyes for a moment and imagined that he was back beside his father in the prow of a dragon ship. A fierce longing for the sea rose up inside of him. Perhaps the gods could do that for him. Perhaps they could bring him to the sea.

'I'd prefer that to Valhalla,' he muttered. His father had told him that all warriors killed with their sword in their hand went to Valhalla. 'It is a great hall full of the gods and everyone is feasting. There is no end to the food and drink,' his father had told him, but Harald had little interest in huge meals and casks of wine and beer. He wanted to be out on the sea again. He almost felt as if he were. He licked his lips. Yes, he was right; there was salt on his lips.

'The sea is not far away!' he said shaking his head to clear the dreamy feeling of faintness. 'If only I could get a boat and I could sail back to the Isle of Man.' All thoughts of Nessa suddenly went from his head. 'I must get back to the Isle of Man,' he said grimly. 'I must take my father's place and lead his men into battles.' He thought of the fleet of dragon ships and pictured himself standing at the prow of the foremost ship, shouting orders, and for a moment that vision blotted out the sadness of his father's terrible death. A new surge of energy rose up inside of him. He crawled another few steps. In front of him was a wall of green with the light glinting through it.

In two minutes, Harald managed to push his way through the spiny branches of the blackthorn. He stood for a moment brushing the white blossoms from his hair and looking all around him. He was in a sloping field. Ahead of him was a road leading to flat bog land and beyond that there seemed to be a great forest.

'And beyond that forest is the sea,' he murmured, once again tasting the bitter salt on his lips.

And then he heard a shout from the little lane that led to the bog.

Chapter 13

Harald had been a warrior among warriors since the age of ten years. He had fought on land and on sea. His life and the life of those around him often depended on his speedy reactions. Instantly he dropped to the ground. The shout came again: 'Lochlann', but this time there was an uncertain note in it. It was a woman's voice – an old woman's voice. Harald stayed very still. She would probably think she had imagined seeing Lochlann, he thought contemptuously. He had no great opinion of old women.

'Lochlann!' the shout came again, but this time it was a bit nearer. Cautiously he peered through the grasses. He could see her now. It was the woman who had come to the house – Old Bridget they had called her. He had seen her plainly while she had been examining Nessa's mother.

'Thor seize her,' he muttered after a minute.

The old woman had jumped off the back of her fat little horse and tied him to the branch of an ash tree. Quickly she pushed her way through a gap in the hedge and then he could see her again puffing and panting as she struggled up the steep slope, her wizened old hand shielding her eyes against the glare of the noontime sun.

I hope she doesn't know about the tunnel, thought Harald. He looked around him in desperation for something to distract her. A grey crow was sitting on an apple tree at the top of the hill. He felt around for a missile. His hand closed over a stone lying at the roots of the blackthorn bushes. With deadly accuracy, and without raising his head, he spun the stone through the air and hit the bird. There was an indignant squawk, the woman's head turned sharply, and in that instant Harald slid back into the tunnel.

★ ★ ★

Fintan's cart stood outside the door of the cottage. Aoife's body lay on it. Nessa turned her eyes away. She had to remain strong; she could not break down and weep.

'Sit on the car, Nessa,' said Fintan.

Nessa shook her head. I must make sure he doesn't take the stallion away again, thought Nessa. The stallion is Harald's only chance of escape.

'No,' she said, shuddering and shaking her head violently. 'I will ride the stallion.' Quickly she turned towards the forge. Fintan followed her hurriedly.

'He'll throw you, Nessa. I'll ride him and you can sit behind me,' he said bravely. The only time that Fintan had ridden the stallion it had thrown him to the ground after a few minutes. 'He's too much for you', he said protectively.

'I can manage him, Fintan,' she said impatiently. 'He's used to me. I want to ride him. I've often ridden him. Don't fuss,' she added hearing her voice rise with a note of hysteria.

The healer looked sharply at her and made a sign with his hand to Fintan. Fintan stepped back and Nessa swung herself onto the stallion's back, patting and stroking his neck and murmuring to him.

Nessa thought about Harald all the way to the graveyard. From time to time a great wave of guilt came over her when she realised that she was thinking so much about the Viking boy. She felt guilty about everything – guilty about her mother, and how underneath the sorrow there was almost a sense of relief, guilty about her father that she had not mourned him enough, guilty about her brother, Lochlann, and guilty about Fintan that suddenly Harald was of more importance to her. The stallion carried her carefully at a walking pace. She felt grateful to him for that; often she had seen him toss his head and bolt if her father was not paying full attention, but now it almost seemed as if the animal understood the turmoil in her mind. Her head drooped and her hands slackened their grip on the bridle. She felt sick and weak.

'Ride on ahead, Colm,' said Niall to the young lad. 'Make sure that the priest is waiting for us when we arrive.' She heard him whisper something to the healer and then the healer said aloud: 'The sooner it's all over and behind her, the sooner her mind will heal.'

So the healer thought there was something the matter with her mind, thought Nessa. Well, perhaps there was. Perhaps she, too, would go mad and start shrieking like her mother. And then she thought of Harald and smiled slightly to herself as she remembered his words to her: 'You have such courage, Nessa,' he had said to her. 'You are braver than any man in battle.' I must go on being brave, I must keep my wits about me and get him safely off to Limerick, she thought, and turned around to smile at Fintan's troubled face.

'You can see that I can ride the stallion, Fintan,' she said. 'He gives me no trouble at all.'

'Only a little bit more to go,' replied Fintan looking at her uneasily. 'We're past Ballinacurra now.'

Nessa turned to look at Clogher – the island everyone called it. Clogher was a small hill rising out of a marsh about a mile north west of Drumshee. It had once been a monastic settlement with a round tower, but now nothing remained but a stump of the tower and one small church beside the graveyard. The priest was already there; Nessa could see his white stole fluttering in the slight breeze on the top of the hill as he came down to meet them.

The priest's face was shocked. I suppose it's not often that he buries two members of the same family in the same week, thought Nessa wearily. She turned her face away from him and rode on up towards the graveyard. She could hear Niall murmuring to him and then the healer's slow solemn voice. She dismounted and tied the stallion to the iron post by the ruined remains of the round tower. The rain began to fall, thick and soft.

'Help Fintan with the grave, Colm,' said Niall aloud. 'Nessa, come into Father Patrick's house out of the rain. You can wait there until all is ready.'

They do not want me to watch while they open the grave, thought Nessa. My father is there and they are afraid that they might uncover him by accident. Without warning, the tears began to pour down her face. Somehow, the death of her father suddenly seemed to be more tragic than that of her mother. He had been such a cheerful, happy, noisy man – she could just see him with his black curly hair and his sparkling blue eyes. He had filled the hillside of Drumshee with song and laughter and with mighty strokes of the hammer on the iron and stone.

'Go indoors, Nessa,' said Niall, taking her arm and guiding her into the priest's house.

'Get her a drink,' murmured the healer to the priest.

'Drink this,' said Father Patrick. He dipped a mug into a pot of hot water and stirred in a spoon of honey.

'Add this to it,' said the healer. He took a small clay pot from his pouch and scooped some white paste from it and added it to the hot water.

'Drink this,' he repeated handing the mug to her.

Nessa drank obediently although by now her sobs almost choked her. The drink was sweet and comforting. She put down the mug on the small rough table.

'Sit here,' said the priest and she sat on his chair by the fire. After a few minutes she was glad to be seated because a great wave of sleepiness seemed to creep over her. She closed her eyes. There must have been something in that white paste, was her last thought as her head nodded forward and she slept until Fintan's voice said in her ear:

'Nessa, wake up, we are going to bury your mother.'

'What!' Nessa struggled to her feet, her thoughts whirling. The ground seemed to rock slightly under her feet. Fintan put his arm around her and she stood there unsteadily for a moment looking into his dark brown eyes. Had they really dug the grave so quickly? Or had she slept for longer than she thought? She did not know and she did not have the energy to ask him. She moved forward hesitantly, glad of his supporting arm. The priest had gone ahead and so had the healer. As they walked across the hilltop she could see a cluster of people standing by the open grave. Her mother's body had already been lowered down into it and for a moment she almost cried out. Quickly she bent down and picked a small bunch of yellow marsh marigolds – kingcups, her mother used to call them. She stood at the graveside and threw them down on to the swathed body. And then someone standing beside her threw another bunch of flowers down.

Nessa turned. It was Old Bridget. At least one of the neighbours is here, she thought. Her throat was swollen and dry and she could not join in the prayers and the responses, but Bridget's voice rose up, riding over all the other voices, galloping through the words almost as though she wanted to force the service to a quick end.

The priest had hardly made the final sign of the cross before Bridget turned to Nessa.

'The boy is out!' she said. Nessa stared at her stupidly. Bridget took her arm and shook her impatiently. 'He's out,' she said. 'Lochlann is out in the fields. What happened? Is he better? Why is he not here with you?'

'What!' exclaimed Fintan from behind her. 'What did you say, Bridget? Lochlann! Did you see Lochlann?'

'Lochlann,' chimed in Niall leaving the priest's side and hurrying over towards them. 'Did you see the boy? Are you sure that you saw the boy,' he asked sharply, staring at Bridget.

Nessa shut her eyes in despair. What had happened? Why had Harald gone out? Was he mad? Was Bridget dreaming? She wished that she could just say simply: 'Lochlann is dead.' But if she said that she would condemn Harald.

'Of course I'm sure,' Bridget was saying indignantly. 'Don't I know the boy well? I've known him since the day that he was born. I saw him as clearly as I see yourself, Niall.'

'Nessa,' said Fintan urgently. 'Did you hear? Bridget says she saw Lochlann.'

'She couldn't have,' said Nessa flatly, turning away. She was conscious that the healer's curious eyes were fixed on her face. She did not want him looking into her eyes. She had an uneasy feeling that he might be able to read her thoughts.

'The boy disappeared last night,' explained Niall. 'We think that he had a fever in the brain. He just got up and walked out of the house. We thought he might be many miles from here by now.'

'Well, I saw him up on the field near the Togher Road,' said Bridget stubbornly.

'Perhaps he's dead,' said Nessa in a low voice. 'Perhaps you have the second sight. Perhaps you saw his spirit.' It gave her a small glimmer of hope to see how the others, even the priest, stared dubiously at Bridget. She did look like someone who might have second sight. No one knew exactly how old she was and some of her cures were only whispered about behind closed doors.

'The girl's not well,' said Bridget. 'What are you talking about? Of course, I saw him. He was up there outside the bushes in your field, just below the wall of the fort. I saw him there.'

'Well the first thing to do is to go back to

Drumshee,' said Niall decisively. He spoke to the healer in a low voice. The healer nodded and turned to follow the priest into the small house beside the church. 'Fintan, leave the cart here – you can pick it up later on. We must get back immediately and see if we can find him. If he is nowhere near to Drumshee then I'll go back and get some of my men out looking for him, but first we must check around his own home. That would be the place that he might wander back to if he is brain-sick.'

He'll be in the tunnel, thought Nessa. No one but I myself is left alive who knows the secret of Drumshee. No one knows of the underground room and the tunnel that leads out on to the Togher field. Suddenly all trace of sleepiness left her. It was as if the danger that Harald stood in had sponged out from her brain the last dregs of the drug that the healer had put in her drink. She allowed a slight smile to come to her lips.

'Lochlann,' she breathed looking at Niall. 'Do you think he has really come back? Perhaps he is cured. Oh, I can hardly dare to hope.'

Niall patted her on the arm. 'We'll get him back for you,' he promised, helping her to mount the grey stallion. 'I'm sure that he is somewhere near to the house. We'll find him.'

'He ran away when he saw me,' snorted Bridget. 'One minute he was there beside the bushes and then he was gone.'

'Perhaps he was ashamed that he had gone away and left me alone with my dead mother,' said Nessa still looking trustingly at Niall. 'Perhaps he didn't want to have to explain things to Bridget before he saw me.' She was astonished to hear herself lie so fluently. Bridget looked annoyed and insulted; that couldn't be helped. The important thing was that Niall cast a glance at Bridget and seemed to think that he would not want to encounter her if he had anything to be ashamed of. He made up his mind swiftly.

'Let Nessa ride ahead,' he said. 'Fintan, you follow at a distance, but not too near. The rest of us will stay behind Fintan. We'll check the lands of Drumshee before we go too far.'

The soft rain continued to fall as they rode the mile between Clogher and Drumshee. From time to time Nessa glanced up at the sky. Yes, she thought, at last some luck was coming her way. The rain was getting less and less – it was just a mist now, but the sky was no longer visible and even the cattle in the fields were just looming shapes. Fog was closing in all around them. Niall would not send his men out hunting for a missing boy in mist like this. Quite soon it would be dangerous even to ride.

If she could divert them away from the fort, and keep them busy searching down by the river then Harald could be saved. Quickly Nessa tapped the stallion with her heels. He responded instantly, quickening his pace, and from behind her she heard Fintan urge on his old horse. That was all right. She would need them all around her in a minute. Over and over again she practised her words.

As soon as they came within sight of the Togher field, Nessa slowed up her horse and waited until Bridget's fat pony came puffing and blowing up beside her.

'Where did you see him, Bridget?' she asked innocently.

'Just up there,' said Bridget. To Nessa's satisfaction she pointed, not at the bushes around the exit from the tunnel, but to a small clump of trees further up the field. Once again Nessa quickened her pace to make sure that she was the first to arrive.

'Lochlann, Lochlann,' she shouted. I'll count up to ten, she reminded herself. The pause seemed very long to her, but she forced herself to wait. She sucked in a deep breath and then suddenly screamed at the top of her voice, 'Lochlann, Lochlann. Oh look! There he is. Look, he is over there!'

'Where? Where?' Niall, Colm and Fintan were at

her side in an instant.

'There!' she screamed pointing towards the river. 'Look! I saw something move over there. He is running down towards the river. That must be his head there just above the hedge.' And then she clicked her heels to the stallion's sides and was off galloping down towards the river.

And after that it was a simple matter. All she had to do was to keep shouting 'Lochlann!' and to keep galloping in different directions across meadows and down beside the river. The fog was getting thicker and thicker, and from time to time, she heard a shout as one of the horses missed footing on the uneven ground.

'Nessa,' shouted Niall after about a quarter of an hour. 'We must stop now. We'll have to lead the horses back up the hill. This is dangerous.'

Obediently Nessa slid to the ground and took the bridle of stallion. She walked over in the direction of his voice. 'You're right,' she said, noting with satisfaction that her voice sounded weary and depressed. 'Follow me,' she added. 'I know the ground well. Keep on my track. We'll walk back up the hill to the fort.' She glanced around at the little group. There was Niall, Colm and Fintan. She frowned. 'Where is Bridget?' she asked.

'She didn't come,' said Fintan. 'I think that she went towards the house.'

Chapter 14

As Nessa trudged silently up the hill leading the stallion ahead of the others her mind was frantically scouring through all her memories of Bridget. Bridget was old; there was no doubt about that. But was she so old that she knew everyone's secrets? Was there ever a time, back in the past – perhaps back in the time of her grandparents, or even her great-grandparents – when someone from Drumshee might have said: 'We have a secret underground room here'? If so, Bridget might by now have discovered Harald. And if she had ... well, Harald had killed before – he had boasted of that – perhaps he might have killed Bridget. Perhaps, though, Bridget would wait until they arrived back and then she would tell of the underground room. And then it would be Harald who would be killed, unless he could still act the part of a silent Lochlann. Unlikely, thought Nessa. Whatever about Fintan and Colm, Niall was a tough, battle-hardened soldier. He would find it unbelievable that a boy, who could walk out of a house and stay out in the fog and rain for hours, was still suffering from a fever. No, she thought. Niall would be suspicious. He might well get the truth out of Harald.

'Did ye find him?' Bridget's voice came floating down as Nessa emerged from the mist and led her horse through the iron gates. Bridget was standing by the cottage door and from behind her came the pungent smell of burning turf. She had lit the fire. So Bridget had just gone into the house, lit the fire, and waited there for them to come back! The anxious thudding of Nessa's heart slowed down and her voice was normal when she spoke.

'No,' she said, conscious of the need to make her voice sound disappointed. 'No, we couldn't find him.'

'I'll go back and get some men,' said Niall, but he did not sound enthusiastic.

'No,' said Nessa. 'You will never find him in that mist. He could be two feet away and you would not see him. There is something wrong with him; I know that. I don't think he is mad or anything like that. I know he is not. I think the sight of Brian Boru's death has so upset him that he . . .' she sought for inspiration and finished, 'that he is not himself. If everyone goes away now and leaves me here by myself, he might come home.'

'There's sense in that,' said Niall, and she could hear the relief in his voice.

'I'll stay here with you,' announced Bridget with a

quick look at the billowing fog outside and then another look at the blazing fire inside the little house.

'No, no,' said Nessa. 'I want to stay here by myself. Lochlann won't come if he hears or sees anyone else. Don't you think?' she added with an appealing look at Niall. He nodded understandingly.

'Will you be all right, by yourself?' asked Fintan. His face looked worried and she felt sorry that she caused him so much pain and anxiety.

'Yes,' she said firmly.

'But . . .' he turned to Niall.

'She's been able to cope with far worse over all those weeks,' said Niall.

Nessa knew what he meant. It was true. An immense weariness came over her when she thought of all those nights and days when she had struggled to drag her mother out of the dark cloud of madness.

'I must stay here by myself,' she repeated.

'Bridget, we'll see you safely to your own front door,' said Niall firmly. 'Colm, help Bridget onto her pony and then you can lead it. I'll take your horse and my own.'

And then they were gone through the gates into the mist and only Fintan was left.

'I hate leaving you,' he said.

'Would you do something for me, Fintan,' she said. 'Would you check on the sheep and the lambs down by the Isle of Maain – and the cows, too. They don't need feeding or anything. The grass is growing well now. And could you check them again tomorrow morning. If Lochlann doesn't come – and now I'm not even sure that I saw him, or that Bridget saw him – but if he doesn't come, then I think I will sleep late tomorrow morning. Come over in the afternoon.'

He said no more, just kissed her and then took his horse. The flat land of the Isle of Maain was between Drumshee and Lough Fergus. He could check on the animals easily when he checked their own. The lands of both farms shared a boundary down there beside the bog.

After Fintan had gone Nessa forced herself to wait. Her first instinct was to rush out, to pull up the flagstone, and to release Harald from the damp cold prison. Don't be stupid, she told herself sternly. Wait! Give them time to get well away. There was no sun so it was hard to estimate how time was passing. Nessa put a fresh sod of turf on the fire and watched it carefully, allowing it to blaze up, then to settle into a glowing red shape in the heart of the fire, and then to collapse into soft brown ash. Only then did she allow herself to get up, to go out into the enclosure, over to the gate, and to listen intently. There was no sound to be heard. The fog deadened everything. She could not even hear the busy sound of the river below the hill.

Then she turned back and went towards the forge with a rushlight in her hand. The flagstone came up easily and her heart leaped with relief. He was there. The rushlight glowed in the darkness, and he was there sitting on a tub and smiling at her.

'I thought you were going to leave me here for ever,' he said. His voice was light and teasing.

'You nearly got yourself caught,' said Nessa sternly. 'Why did you let Old Bridget see you?'

He ignored that and started to climb up the steps. His leg seemed better, she thought. He had probably been exercising it and the strength was coming back into it.

'Come quickly,' she said softly. 'Come into the warmth.'

'Give me a kiss first,' he said teasingly.

'Hush,' she whispered. 'Men have been out looking for you. You were lucky that the fog came.'

He laughed. Everything seemed to be a joke to him. He was in high spirits. He reached out and patted the stallion as he passed and the stallion permitted it. Then he walked towards the cottage with only a slight limp.

'A fire,' he said delightedly, his voice still alarmingly loud. 'This is just what I was dreaming of!'

'You must eat now,' she said. 'I have only bread and cheese, but I do have some ale.'

So she cut thick slices of bread, spread them with butter and then sliced a small goat's cheese. She poured the ale with a steady hand and then sat down beside him, watching him eat.

'What happened?' he asked with his mouth full.

'We buried my mother,' she answered. Her voice was quite steady, she noticed. Somehow the terrible sorrow of her mother's death seemed to move back into her mind; she had shut it out. I'll think about it in a few days' time, she thought hurriedly, and continued aloud: 'Then Bridget came and said that she had seen you. So they hunted for you, but luckily the fog came. They still think you are Lochlann.'

He laughed delightedly, crunched the last of the bread and cheese between his splendid white teeth, tossed back the ale, and turned to her.

'You must go now,' said Nessa turning away from the look in his eyes and busying herself with packing some bread and cheese into a leather satchel for the journey ahead of him.

'In a minute,' he said, absent-mindedly running his finger around and around a knot on the ancient wood of the kitchen table.

Nessa waited. There was more to be said; she knew that.

'Come with me, Nessa,' he said abruptly. 'Come back to the Isle of Man with me. Come and be my wife. I love you, and you love me,' he finished lifting his head with an arrogant gesture.

She shook her head. 'No,' she said. 'No, I couldn't.'

'What difference does it make that you are Irish and I am Viking?' he demanded though she had not said that, had not even thought that. 'We love each other. You will be happy with me. My father had many ships and many acres of land. I am his only son. I will give you everything that you have ever dreamed of.'

'We have only one horse,' she said weakly.

He laughed at that. 'The grey stallion will carry us both.'

She nodded. That was true. The grey stallion had borne the weight and bulk of Oscar without ever slackening his speed; She and Harald would be only half that burden.

'You'll come then?' he laughed with delight. His blue eyes shone and his white teeth flashed with the smile. He was the most beautiful thing that Nessa had ever seen.

'No,' she said again and then added: 'I love Fintan

and I am going to marry him.'

After she had said the words, she wondered whether they were true. But they were the only words that would convince him; she knew that.

And then there was silence between them and the silence grew and it lengthened and it filled the little house. And there was no more to be said. The decision had been made and it would not be changed. Never would Nessa know what life would have held for her on that far-away island of the Isle of Man if she had said 'Yes'. They stood, one on either side of the table, and looked at each other.

And then the door opened and in came Fintan.

He stared from one to the other. It seemed to Nessa that the boy had become a man. He said nothing. The boy Fintan would have asked a dozen questions, would have made a dozen explanations for his return, but this man just looked at her and looked at the blond boy on the other side of the table. He understood; she knew that. Somehow in his love for her, the truth had been unveiled to him.

'It's not Lochlann, is it,' he stated calmly. 'You knew he was not Lochlann.'

Nessa did not answer. Across the table from her, Harald grew very still. She saw his eyes flicker down towards the knife in his belt, but he made no effort to grasp it. Fintan wore a sword at his waist and, though not as tall as Harald, his muscles were developed by long years of work at the blacksmith's forge.

'Who are you?' asked Fintan. And then after a moment he added, 'He doesn't understand our language, does he?' Nessa nodded. Harald gave a careless shrug. He understands some of our language, thought Nessa.

'We brought back a Viking, that was it, wasn't it?' continued Fintan. 'I remember your mother saying that it wasn't Lochlann and we didn't believe her.'

Harald turned his eyes away from Fintan and held out his hand to Nessa.

'What does he want?' asked Fintan. There was no anger and no jealousy in his tone.

'Tell him what I have offered you,' challenged Harald. 'You will live like a queen. I have many ships. When I go a-viking I will bring you back many gifts. I will build you a house like a palace; I will load your arms with bracelets, your neck with collars of gold. You will sit on silken cushions and have slaves to do your bidding.'

She stared at Harald. She did not move for a moment, but then slowly, and finally, she shook her head.

Harald stood up and he walked to the door. Then he turned, came back and kissed her on the lips. He cast one quick glance at Fintan and then went through the door and out into the night. They heard the neigh of the stallion, answered by Fintan's horse, and then there was a clop-clop on the stones. And then there was silence.

'He wanted you to go with him,' stated Fintan eventually.

'Yes,' said Nessa.

'But you did not want to?'

Nessa thought for a moment. 'I said "no",' she answered eventually.

Fintan, in his turn, thought about that for a moment. It wasn't the same thing; he knew that. He opened his lips to question, but then shut them again.

'So we'll be married in June?' he queried.

She hesitated, and then nodded. It was the right decision; there was no doubt about that. She and Fintan would be right together. He would take over the blacksmith's business; she would help with the farm. They would have children and Drumshee would be a happy place once more as it was when she and Lochlann were growing up.

'Fintan, I am very tired now. I would like to sleep,' she said gently. 'Will you come back in the morning? We will talk then.'

He smiled. He did not kiss her, but she did not expect or want that.

'Don't come to the door,' he said. 'It's a bad night. Sleep well.'

She sank down beside the fire but a moment later she was roused by an exclamation.

'He's taken my horse!' shouted Fintan as he burst back into the cottage.

Nessa went to the door and looked out. The grey stallion was still there where she had left him, tied to the ring outside the forge.

'You take the stallion,' she said wearily.

Fintan shook his head. 'No,' he said. 'It's a treacherous night for riding. The fog is worse than ever. I won't risk him. I'll walk back. I'll be just as quick; I had to go at walking pace most of the way over. Go inside to the fire, sweetheart. I'll be over at noon so you sleep as much as you want to.'

Nessa stayed at the door, though, until the sound of his footsteps were swallowed up by the thick swathes of fog. Then she went in and came out with a bowlful of oats. She held the bowl in her hand while the stallion bent his noble head and ate the oats greedily. She was glad that he was left to her; the smell of his hide brought back memories of her father. As a child she had often ridden, held safely in his arms, on the back of the stallion. She put down the bowl and put her arms around the stallion's neck and he nuzzled her hair.

'I'd better untie you, boy,' she murmured. Carefully she took off the bridle and turned the stallion loose in the Cathaireen field. Then she went back, picked up the wooden bowl, and she went indoors. It was just as she was putting the bowl back on to the shelf that her hand struck a small hard roll. She picked it up and stared at it. She was puzzled for a moment, but then she remembered: it was the letter and the brooch that the Queen of Scotland had sent her.

She unrolled the little scroll of vellum, put the beautiful brooch to one side on the table and then settled down to read the letter again.

You must be a very beautiful young girl … I have told your brother that he should take you to Kincora where you will meet many people and take part in the fun and festivities there. You must enjoy your youth! Your brother and your father should find someone to care for your mother so that your happiness is not sacrificed. I'm sure that my father and my brothers would welcome you at Kincora. Bring this letter with you and show it when you arrive there.

And Nessa sat beside the slow-dying fire with the letter in her hand.

epilogue

It was Christmas time at Kincora. Brian Boru had been mourned and now, although he was never to be forgotten, Kincora had put aside the mourning and the hall was filled with the light of a hundred candles of beeswax. Teige, his eldest surviving son, was now king and there was to be a great banquet to thank all of the clans for their help at Clontarf.

The tables were covered with white linen cloths and spread with great bowls of bread, platters of roasted fowl, huge joints of steaming pork, of venison and of beef. There were nuts piled high in woven baskets, large balls of cows' milk cheese and small round cheeses of goat's milk, jugs foaming with ale and flagons brimming with dark red wine.

The king had not yet arrived to take his place at the table so all the members of his court and all of the visitors lined the sides of the banqueting hall. The man who came to the door, travel-stained and weary, was almost blinded by the colours of purple, crimson and yellow *léinte* embroidered with bronze or silver threads. His eye went to a group of woman by the high table. These would be the ladies of the court of Kincora, he guessed and he thought they looked like clusters of orchids in the meadows in June. Gold earrings dangled from their ears and their hair, red, brown or black, flashed with gold ornaments. His eye passed over all of these and then stopped. Yes, she was there. There was no mistaking the Viking-blond hair. He pushed his way through the crowd.

She was looking older, he thought, taller, too. She had changed in other ways, as well. She had always been beautiful, but her beauty, when he had seen her last, had been overlaid with the shadow of sorrow, anxiety and terrible tension. Now it shone forth more brightly than that of any other woman there. Now, he sensed, she was in command of herself and knew what she wanted from life. His eye swept admiringly over her, taking in the blue *léine* that exactly matched her eyes and the purple *brat* wrapped around her tall figure and pinned at the shoulder with a magnificent brooch made from gold and studded with rubies.

'Nessa, you're looking wonderful,' he greeted her warmly.

For a moment she hardly knew him. He sensed that her life back at Drumshee was now far away from her. Then her face lit up.

'Niall,' she said. 'Niall of Corcomroe.'

'I bear a message,' said Niall.

She held out her hand, but he shook his head.

'It's not a written message,' he said. 'It's from Fintan. He can't write.'

The creamy pallor of her face flushed. Of course, the message would be from Fintan and, of course, he could not write; she knew that. She should have remembered that. Suddenly a terrible sense of shame filled her.

'I left him a letter on the kitchen table when I left Drumshee,' she murmured. 'I had forgotten that he could not read or write. I could not think that morning. I just took the grey stallion and I went.'

'He brought your letter to me,' said Niall. 'I read it to him. I told him about the Queen of Scotland and her invitation to you to go to Kincora. I told him that you wanted him to have the farm and the forge for his own. He's looked after it for you,' he added when she said nothing. 'Drumshee has never looked better. All the animals are well.'

'I knew he would,' she said softly. 'I knew I could trust him.'

'He told me everything. He told me about the Viking boy also,' said Niall, watching her narrowly.

The flush on her face faded.

'He was nothing,' she said indifferently. 'He has gone back to his own land, I suppose. I should have waited to see Fintan, though. I should have told him myself'

Niall shook his head. 'I think you did the right thing,' he said. 'I talked to the healer about it. He made me understand. You needed to get away. You needed to rest your mind and to get away from the sorrow. I sent a messenger to Kincora to see if you had got there safely so I was able to put Fintan's mind at rest. He wanted to go himself, but I said no. Give her time, I said.'

He looked at her for a moment and then he laughed. 'It was not easy for him, of course,' he said with amusement. 'The hills around Drumshee were ringing night and day with ironstone being smashed by his hammer. You should see his muscles now!'

She laughed, too. A faint pink tinged her cheeks again and her blue eyes glowed. Niall gave a small grunt of satisfaction, and she flushed a deeper pink.

'And you've heard nothing from the Viking boy since?' he asked looking at her closely. She shook her head.

'He sent back Fintan's horse, you know,' said

Niall with a chuckle. 'A man from Limerick brought it back to Fintan. He said that Harold had got back safely to the Isle of Man. Harold told the man to say that he hoped Fintan was not as slow as his horse!'

Nessa laughed. There was no shade of embarrassment in her manner. Niall watched her carefully and gave a satisfied nod to himself.

'May I give my message now?' he asked. 'I won't stay for this banquet. I want to get home to my own fireside and to my own wife and children for Christmas.'

'Yes,' she said softly. 'Give your message and I'll give my answer.'

'I think you know what the message is,' he said looking at her keenly. 'Can you give me your answer now?'

'Tell him . . .' she said hesitantly, 'tell him that I will be back in the spring. Tell him I will be there when the first kingcups bloom in the fields at Drumshee.'